C000269060

TAIL OF THE TANIWHA

A Collection of Short Stories

Beatnik

Beatnik Publishing

PO Box 8276, Symonds Street, Auckland 1150, New Zealand

First published in 2016 by Beatnik Publishing.

Text: © 2016 Courtney Sina Meredith
Design and Typesetting: © 2016 Beatnik Design Ltd.
Creative Director: Sally Greer
Designer: Kyle Ranudo
Production Manager: Kitki Tong
Typeface: Ashbury
Type Designer: Dieter Hofrichter

Photography: Sally Greer

This book is copyright. Apart from any fair dealing for the purposes of private study, research or review, as permitted under the Copyright Act, no part may be reproduced by any process without the permission of the publishers.

Printed and bound in China.

ISBN 978-0-9922648-9-5

TAIL
of the
TANIWHA

Courtney Sina Meredith

For my mother, Kim Meredith Melhuish.

CONTENTS

Great Works — 8
A/B — 14
Ibu & Tufuga — 30
Aotahi — 32
The Coconut King — 46
Taniwha House — 52
Manifesto — 68
Perfumed Stars — 78
Hundred — 82
The Youthful Dead — 84
Leaning Trees — 90
X — 108
Patriarch, Eldest Son, Ghost Son, Daughter — 114
Corner of Bleibtreu — 124
Dreams — 130
Old Friend — 136
25 — 138
'New Zealand you' — 144

She has a topknot of black curls, a trench in charcoal and a white linen tunic that stops at her knees to reveal black tights running into leather boots with gold points. Her notebook is chocolate brown; she takes it from her handbag and continues quietly the conversation with the deity Nafanua, a waterfall of indecipherable pleas running down the page. Inside the Tate Modern, she walks softly and quickly in search of the Henri Matisse exhibition – *The Cut-Outs*, a period when Matisse began *cutting* and *carving* into colour.

'Oh there you are... great goddess, I'm here, finally, in front of The Snail. Yes, the shapes and the colours are nice but what the fuck? I don't see a snail!' She shifts her weight to the left hoping for a better view, and even slips the handbag over from her right shoulder into her hands, expecting a miracle.

'Nope,' she says under her breath, people close by beginning to stare. 'No damn snail anywhere.'

She thinks back to that day in Albert Park with Jan, trying her best to understand criminal law. 'All of the material facts you have to pick out, the precedent or whatever, it's like freaking soup in my head. How am I supposed to remember all of this stuff? And why are the criminals always brown? I mean, the whole idea of justice is just a bit cracked. You have these rich lawyers right? They need crime to have a job, like the police – right? If there were no criminals they'd be out of work and hungry! Or maybe they'd be policing real things like oil rigs in the sea, and predators of endangered birds, and acid rain on heritage buildings–'

'Stop it, surrender, you're just out of your depth, Ake.' That was Jan, laughing carelessly, running a hand through her blonde mane.

'When I read a case at home, it's with a Krispie and a cup of tea. When *you* read a case it's at your dad's firm, with his partners connecting the dots for you.'

Jan had glared back at her, but eventually they both laughed and headed for the pub.

'Nafanua, are you still there? I think of all the times you must have felt unsure but you stayed fierce and you kept fighting.' By now there was only a rainbow blob and she'd stopping trying to make out any creature, deciding it was a test.

'There was one paper I took in security studies for politics. I read about the power that shapes simple things, like the direction I'm writing in (left to right). One tutor made us all wear masks down the main road to see how it felt to be different. It didn't feel any different to walking down the street with my own face.'

She surveys the white walls slowly, admires a blue form, considers a snow flower, absorbing strange-looking bodies brought to life at the edge of death. Plinth after plinth a new definition of living unfurls. Nafanua is nowhere to be seen.

'Am I the negress? That idea of exotica, beautiful, two-dimensional. This is important, it was important to Matisse. I mean, it might be okay to be a monster, an attraction for a while, but the novelty... it wouldn't take long to wear off. If I had to be quoted either way, I would stay the path of denouncement. They put us up on walls because we *are* works of art, but it's the wrong way round, Nafanua – they think they're looking at us.'

She writes with a sleek new pen given to her the day after she arrived in this huge, strange city. He was Polish, the banker; he opened an account for her on Edgeware Road. She didn't feel bad taking the pen – there were plenty in a glass jar on his desk and she noticed airline tickets. 'Canary Islands,' he said proudly in a thick accent. 'Don't worry, you'll get used to it here. You miss home at first, then slowly London becomes an even better home.' His teeth were shiny white, like he'd smeared them in Vaseline.

Everybody said she had to do the Tate – her boss, her work friends and even her aunty Sia who'd clutched her tightly by the airport departure gate: 'Go to the Tate, especially the show of a master. My mate Emma said it's amazing. The food and the gift shop are really good too!' Akenese had promised she would go. Her family looked smaller, fanned out in a semicircle, waving goodbye. She could see the shared features, how they mirrored each other, wide-eyed with excitement. It would've killed her cousin Lisia to know that from a distance she looked like she belonged too. A part of Ake wanted to run back to her grandma and plead with her not to die while she went off to 'find herself' just like the girls she used to mock at university, especially Jan who had somehow become family. She suddenly wanted to be from the generation before, cheering safely from the sidelines, praying for the future while her daughter, or her daughter's daughter, set out into the world all alone. Her uncles didn't cry but her mother shed a few tears, standing in the centre, shimmering, coming to the fore and disappearing all at once. Akenese remembers the great pang in her chest when she finally walked through to customs, unsure of when she would see them all again.

A well-dressed businessman enters the Tate Modern to see Kazimir Malevich's first retrospective in thirty years. His thin black glasses give an older appearance but under his arm a lustrous snakeskin folder suggests something else. On the way to contemplate drawings and sculptures he takes in the Blue Nude (ll) observed by a woman ten metres long, or so she appears in a crisp linen dress not showing her legs, scribbling into a leather journal. He looks at her in profile, considers the difference between women who witness and women who observe.

Akenese can feel his gaze, but continues in her notebook – *writing is a lot of watching*. Her hands flashes across the page. She can fit into the scene around her if she just keeps herself busy enough, if she can just capture the moment for Aunty Sia. It will be as the polite Polish banker believed, slowly an even better home. She arches her feet inside her boots, takes care to keep them flat – the small hole under the right sole lets in a chill.

Ake ruminates over her mother's warning: 'You have to

notice the subtle changes when you get out there or else you're going to miss it, Ake. You'll go all the way to London for nothing. Just stop and you'll see things aren't the same, they're layered, multi-layered.'

She stands in front of The Sheaf, completely dwarfed by ideas of how the world could be. Tourists in anoraks move in closer to each other, wetting their lips, approaching with soft greetings – 'Hallo' or 'Ciao' or 'Namaste' – as though people from outside Britain are encouraged to band together for safety. Yellow-haired children drag their feet, tired from all the motionlessness. She senses their urge to break free as one of them blows her a kiss.

'Nafanua, that's another thing. They say children are precious, but the ones here have grown from concrete, out of the shadows, towards a dull sky. I haven't seen the sun in weeks and I'm already starting to feel grey inside. It seems unfair watching them miss out on grass and fresh air and sunlight. I don't know, maybe they grow up faster here and it makes them superior adults. I might've stayed in law school and come out the other end an actual lawyer if I'd grown up somewhere like this.'

She sees him again, moving between columns, takes care to watch him without being noticed. She imagines a world of trading markets and finance. He might have his own firm; who else would have the power to stroll around the gallery so casually this late in the morning? She sends a text to Lisia – *Seeing the Tate in 3D!* When she looks up from her phone he catches her off guard, standing close by, gesturing to her notebook. 'Are you in the arts?'

This is how you shave a decade off your life, she thinks, or maybe this is how you lose your chances altogether. This must be how easy it is to set out on a new journey that becomes an updated version of the past.

Akenese smiles at him. 'The cut-outs were lovely.' She walks out of the Tate with Nafanua assuredly in tow.

Her dark hair catches the afternoon light. Birds overhead are drawn onto the sky by hand.

'She's definitely got something – maybe a touch of Arab?' says the older of the men, breaking the silence.

'She eats jerk chicken, you can tell by her smile,' comes the answer.

They watch her standing among the flowerbeds. Eating meat pies and drawing on rolled cigarettes, both men slacken their tool belts to relax. Another cold morning of kerbs and pipes, commuters passing in great hordes. Nobody smiling or saying hello, the usual, the inevitable. Moving each leg slowly as though they have just been discovered, the men let out tired sighs, shifting about on the park bench. The younger man opens a can of Coke, makes an offering to his workmate, who shakes his head with a strong frown. Both pretend to check their phones while keeping watch on the woman across the way, now writing beside the sculpture.

More people filter into the square, half-expecting rain, desiring sun. At the centre of the garden, the half-timbered hut buzzes with life. A head of golden curls swoops across the lawn and stops mid-flight, coughs into a sleeve before taking off in a brilliant rush.

'She could be Indian, you know?' The younger, eager to continue. 'Nice African hips, mind,' he keeps on, 'or she could be some kind of part-Chinese part-Japanese, something from that region?'

'Whatever she is, I'm liking it,' says the older one, his fingers caressing paper around tobacco.

A group of slight women in soft greens sit cross-legged in the middle of the park, leaning into each other with little white notepads, sketching birds and passers-by. Quarrelling couples hiss profanities, brilliant shapes of youth, throwing their heads back, drinking light, oblivious to their wonder.

Akenese eyes the bronze sculpture, thinks of home and revels in the scene. She takes out her notebook and writes, 'There is a plane tree, not a totara or a pohutukawa but a plane tree. There are two men mending pipes over by the entrance. The younger one talks so loud I can't wait to go home to see if I do look African or like an Indian or even Japanese. You were right, Nafanua, there is only me. At the Tate I saw nothing but myself.'

I wanted to know what you would do to me.
Falling in love was unplanned.

Normal people can do that Midsomer stuff. On
the couch. Eating something hot, not hearing
the rain on the roof right in their pelvic bone.
Thrum, thrum, thrum. Watching Barnaby
solve another mystery, a family man with Joyce
at home waiting for him, reading the paper,
clutching her heart. Everyday people can do
that, but not the raging and the swinging.

I thought, I'll be safe to swim out towards you
just a little, and be the dolphin by the cruise
ship that brings joy. Thinking that afterwards
you'd go down into your cabin with a real man
to undress you with his real hands, not flippers.
And in the night, on the ship, you'd wake from
a dream about being pulled under the waves
and the real man would pat you, saying, 'Hush,
you're safe, there, there.'

The dolphin from before would seem to have
happened long ago; you'd feel certain while
going back to sleep that it never happened
to you. It was a friend; it was a stranger at the
bank – laughing with her son about a rubber
toy bobbing about in the sink.

There's a great story, about a stuffy couple that go away on holiday and while they're driving to their hotel, they run over a child.

You feel a bit terrible for finding so much to relate to up until that point – the dreariness of packing, stuffing your toiletries into a makeup bag, clearing out the fridge, giving the floors a good

vacuum. Lugging all your crap to the airport, checking that you have your passport and your tickets, making sure there isn't anything stupid in your handbag like razor sharp tweezers, a stray lighter or – worse – perfume you'll just have to throw in the bin at customs. Contemplating the strange gift of leaving your life for a few days. Flying somewhere warm to escape the excessive scaffolding that holds in place a person you no longer recognise.

Every inch of skin requires constant preening, plucking, waxing. Merino in winter, linen in summer, everything packed away in the right box for the right season somewhere cool and dry. The jewellery is tasteful, sometimes bright but never bold; your hair needs a certain moisture-rich conditioner and every morning after washing there's the hair dryer blasting, then straightening, then ruffling to make it look as though you spent no time on it at all. Eventually making it to the boardroom in a well-detailed heap, joining in with everyone's traffic complaints, watching as items are handwritten onto the agenda last minute. What's the point of getting everything in on time if you just end up bending the rules anyway, or even snapping them in half?

In the story, I don't remember if the couple felt bad about running over the child. You have to lose something, sacrifice yourself in some way, to get to the 'hotel,' right? Mecca, the Promised Land, whatever it is you've been toiling towards.

Why are you with me? I'm selfish. It's proven.
In my DNA, love. My dad is a seaman; he fucks
off for a living. Should've mentioned when
we met that I'm unreliable but likeable. I'm
not real. I should've said, 'Hey don't mistake
me for someone: I'm no one.' Would that have
changed anything? It's stupid to dwell on the
past but a real man would've fronted up; even
sick men can be real, but I'm an insect, covered
in fallen leaves. A kefe, covered in lies.

Do you remember the tree above us? Twenty
Sundays ago? I said it wasn't the fun type. The
first type. I've got the second type; I said it out
loud, but you weren't listening because you
finally liked something about yourself. In your
own relationship bubble, with another face of
mine. I could see you and him, I was floating
up in the tree and looking down on you both.
He was smiling a big fake smile but he looked
almost happy and I know that you were fooled
because you smiled back with your eyes, for
real. I was balancing on the top branch like
the ninjas in Crouching Tiger, shouting out
to you, 'Hey, girl, protect your heart and the
environment, he's not right in the head, take
your picnic pastries and run!' You pointed up
at me, and the grey man next to you looked
up too, like a dumb caterpillar. Trying to make
shapes out of clouds, he sniffled something
political, disagreed with a trade act he knew
you didn't like. I wasn't fooled. I knew it wasn't
a Hallensteins ad. That guy didn't belong with
a non-caterpillar woman, a real one carrying
the moon around in her arms and legs. 'Hey,
fake-ass kefe,' I was shouting from the treetops.
'Hey, lying scum, she's gonna see right through
you soon enough!'

Why are you still here?

The 40-hour week is full of pricks. You work for them, you work with them, or worse – you accept their money, favours and pardons, so you have to listen to them. Absolute drivel; you'd learn more watching a horse take a shit.

Only coffee and cassava chips make sense to me by the afternoon. Even so, I have to appear clear-headed and ready to take on new challenges at the drop of a hat. Nobody likes a Negative Nancy. Walk it off – better yet, cross-fit those blues into a toned but delicate flower. Start a blog; let it out, just in a smart and constructive way that other women can learn from. They didn't mention that at university, how I'd have to share my success. With every other woman. That everything I do or have done or might pursue in future would come down to how much I am or was or wasn't or could be a woman.

In the new world I'm told to fail forward, lean in, take each day as it comes, accept what I can't change, never give up and on top of that, embrace my setbacks. Every catastrophe has a silver lining, every upset another karmic fruit basket, just beyond my reach, its deliverance dependent on my faith, my ability to believe.

'Don't theorise,' my mother tells me. 'Practice love'.

'Don't rob yourself,' my best friend tells me. 'Stay in the moment.'

Barnaby's smart because he takes his time,
doesn't make rash decisions about who did
it. And he's always got a young guy with him,
stupid; shooting from the hip, ready to pin it
on the first dodgy suspect. Barnaby's like, 'Hey,
mate, pull your head in; it's not this guy, all
right?' Smart, taking his time, taking it all in,
piecing shit together in his head bit by bit. You
need a Barnaby, not an insect.

I've seen the Northern Star bounce off my
claws, when I turned into a bat. A friend of
mine, she had her hands in my fur, trying to
pull me down from the sky. And that's the first
time they put me into a deep sleep; someone
had to watch me for three days non-stop. Took
my razor away, anything sharp, which was
stupid because I was a bat with huge claws and
I could've stabbed them all.

The entire northern sky wheels around
Polaris... But you're here with me, melting
into the carpet. I'm not worth it – I don't solve
crimes and I don't really fly either.

All those stars caught in all that darkness,
swirling around, calculations. Fuck, I wish
you'd known me in my last life. I had my shit
together. I had savings and a dog. You would've
liked me, understood me, in that life. This one
is a bit of a write-off, but the next time around
– it'll be us chasing monsters, reading papers in
a country home. It'll be me patting you back to
sleep when you wake up from a bad dream.

Who knows, you could be right; then again,
you could be the dolphin and I could be the
cruise ship. You could be the bat and I could
be the night sky. I read an article the other day
that reality isn't even a real thing, it's all made
up.

Every theory we've proven has been disproven.
Funny world to be in, right? Making it up as
we go along? I'm not even really here, I'm in
several places at once – or the light is, I guess,
and we're just made of light and water anyway,
so you're not even totally seeing me. You've
decided what you'd like to see. Decided to
yourself that I'm the one? Do I really look
anything like him?

Black licorice dreads. Big mouth. Flat nose.

Of course you don't, it's inconvenient.

Dolphins have superior athletic abilities, they're extremely fit – that's how they're able to jump out of the water and do somersaults and fancy tail walking. Have you ever swum upside down in the water hunting for food? No, I didn't think so. And a bat – really? It's easier for you to believe you're incapable of anything, than it is to try for something. Even a little something is better than a lot of nothing.

I don't see you like that.

Did we move into this apartment because of the location? Or was it the pool?

A bit of both, but you're the one
who swims.

Sure, for a shower after the spa. That's what I
use. The spa.

But we don't look out onto anything! The strip
clubs make you cringe. The glass bank hurts
your eyes. The bakery, we never go there.

You know what I like about this place? The
high ceilings, there's so much space to think.
Come home, drop my things on the floor, and
completely unwind.

Yeah, and wonder about the doughnuts. Cream
doughnuts across the road.

And the gym? Do you ever use the gym?

I moved into this apartment because of the view.

Because it's ugly.

Touch the roof with your chin?

And kill the idea? No way.

You can go and get some, any time.

If I could just remove the apartment blocks across the road, and the carpark over there, I'd be onto something.

Kick out the Italians downstairs, give their African drums to the City Mission, and the bakery - that could go too, it clashes with the fluoro charm of the yoga centre.

Maybe the yoga centre would work better as a supervised gym? Something sophisticated and low key, with a green smoothie bar on the bottom floor.

The bottle shop, I guess it could stay, but it would have to be repainted half black, half white, and the staff replaced by humans and the prices aligned with the supermarkets' - what's fair, what's affordable. But we'd need a hit put out on all those greasy food-cart operators below. Full of sugar and cockroaches. Remove those, and turn the street benches around towards the light. Why they're sitting hidden in the shade of cheap fusion cafés escapes me.

People would stop and drink their coffee, meet up for office lunches, come after work for spin classes and free weights. They'd look up to where I'm looking now.

The view would be amazing.

IBU & TUFUGA

Ibu has made pork and prawn noodle soup. Two loaves
of white bread, one nutty loaf too. The dough rose with the
afternoon sun.

The Tufuga has his sister over from Niu Sila; she wants to
see Hogwarts and ghosts. Her mokopuna lives in New York.

I find a book in the den about thieves. Manu is a good girl
she makes a platter. We eat cheese and crackers and read.

The Tufuga farewells his sister over from Niu Sila, she won't
stay any longer, she misses her mokopuna. She has to pack,
she has to leave, she is sorry.

The local pub is pink with playful bunting; you have
to excuse yourself for walking. In the courtyard, everybody
smokes.

Ibu brings me a cup of chamomile tea. She dyed her hair
brown, she looks different. We plan to go to the markets.

If a bird flies inside it means someone has died, the garden is in heat all the bees buzz. Ibu loves to plant new trees.

The Tufuga is worried about October, he is teaching an Italian history paper. The Tufuga does not speak Italian.

A new delicatessen has opened on North Parade. It sells boutique meats and handmade cheese. Ibu goes to town for the day.

Manu makes a huge jug of Pimms; the neighbours come over without their kids. We sit outside under the bright blue sky.

I show Manu my open wound, seeping every day, seeping love. She says my ex was really hot.

Ibu watches us from the garden table. She knows exactly who I might become, if only the house could house my spirits.

AOTAHI

Te Ikaroa is the Milky Way. Whatever he meant, it made sense to me. You were very small, Aotahi. It's like swimming back to yourself from a great distance. My brother knows a lot about what you should do to keep yourself safe and what might get you hurt.

Te Ikaroa is the Milky Way. They drew pictures of germs crawling all over small bodies. Whatever he meant, it made sense to me. He said no one can hear you when you talk to yourself so it's no good praying with your eyes and mouth closed. You were very small, Aotahi. It's like swimming back to yourself from a great distance. They are together apart, they are unrepeatable moments. My brother knows a lot about what you should do to keep yourself safe and what might get you hurt. Whatever Kaiwaka said to my brother I just smile through my tears.

33

My brother helped Kaiwaka with his learning because Kaiwaka threatened to cut himself otherwise. **Te Ikaroa is the Milky Way.** They drew pictures of germs crawling all over small bodies. **Whatever he meant, it made sense to me.** He said no one can hear you when you talk to yourself so it's no good praying with your eyes and mouth closed. **You were very small, Aotahi. It's like swimming back to yourself from a great distance.** They are together apart, they are unrepeatable moments. **My brother knows a lot about what you should do to keep yourself safe and what might get you hurt.** Whatever Kaiwaka said to my brother I just smile through my tears.

My brother helped Kaiwaka with his learning because Kaiwaka threatened to cut himself otherwise. Te Ikaroa is the Milky Way. They drew pictures of germs crawling all over small bodies. If you go looking for a sign that you're living right, you won't find one. Whatever he meant, it made sense to me. He said no one can hear you when you talk to yourself so it's no good praying with your eyes and mouth closed. You were very small, Aotahi. His wife will decide about whether the dog is a boy or a girl and whether it sleeps inside or out. It's like swimming back to yourself from a great distance. They are together apart, they are unrepeatable moments. My brother knows a lot about what you should do to keep yourself safe and what might get you hurt. Whatever Kaiwaka said to my brother I just smile through my tears.

My brother helped Kaiwaka with his learning because Kaiwaka threatened to cut himself otherwise. My brother was good at colouring in the blank space between words and people. Te Ikaroa is the Milky Way. They drew pictures of germs crawling all over small bodies. If you go looking for a sign that you're living right, you won't find one. Whatever he meant, it made sense to me. He said no one can hear you when you talk to yourself so it's no good praying with your eyes and mouth closed. You were very small, Aotahi. His wife will decide about whether the dog is a boy or a girl and whether it sleeps inside or out. My brother said that everything given is taken away in one go but that it returns to you over time. It's like swimming back to yourself from a great distance. Ruawahia is a star that marks the ninth month. They are together apart, they are unrepeatable moments. My brother knows a lot about what you should do to keep yourself safe and what might get you hurt. Whatever Kaiwaka said to my brother I just smile through my tears.

My brother helped Kaiwaka with his learning because Kaiwaka threatened to cut himself otherwise. My brother was good at colouring in the blank space between words and people. Te Ikaroa is the Milky Way. They drew pictures of germs crawling all over small bodies. Kaiwaka said that god means good orderly direction but my brother told him that god means good onerous deeds and that you have to act god out. If you go looking for a sign that you're living right, you won't find one. Whatever he meant, it made sense to me. He said no one can hear you when you talk to yourself so it's no good praying with your eyes and mouth closed. You were very small, Aotahi. His wife will decide about whether the dog is a boy or a girl and whether it sleeps inside or out. My brother said that everything given is taken away in one go but that it returns to you over time. It's like swimming back to yourself from a great distance. Ruawahia is a star that marks the ninth month. They are together apart, they are unrepeatable moments. My brother knows a lot about what you should do to keep yourself safe and what might get you hurt. Whatever Kaiwaka said to my brother I just smile through my tears. They dance in the same wide opus of darkness and suspended inferno.

Te Tira o Puanga is the light of Orion's belt. My brother helped Kaiwaka with his learning because Kaiwaka threatened to cut himself otherwise. My brother was good at colouring in the blank space between words and people. Te Ikaroa is the Milky Way. They drew pictures of germs crawling all over small bodies. Kaiwaka said that god means good orderly direction but my brother told him that god means good onerous deeds and that you have to act god out. If you go looking for a sign that you're living right, you won't find one. Whatever he meant, it made sense to me. He said no one can hear you when you talk to yourself so it's no good praying with your eyes and mouth closed. You were very small, Aotahi. His wife will decide about whether the dog is a boy or a girl and whether it sleeps inside or out. Other people's brothers would've asked to see the sharp stick that Kaiwaka always talks about and if they were really bored they'd tell him to go on and do it then. My brother said that everything given is taken away in one go but that it returns to you over time. It's like swimming back to yourself from a great distance. Ruawahia is a star that marks the ninth month. My brother and Kaiwaka and the other children need to keep sharing stories and listening to each other. They are together apart, they are unrepeatable moments. My brother knows a lot about what you should do to keep yourself safe and what might get you hurt. Whatever Kaiwaka said to my brother I just smile through my tears. They dance in the same wide opus of darkness and suspended inferno.

He's going to name his children after constellations. Te Tira o Puanga is the light of Orion's belt. My brother helped Kaiwaka with his learning because Kaiwaka threatened to cut himself otherwise. My brother was good at colouring in the blank space between words and people. Te Ikaroa is the Milky Way. They drew pictures of germs crawling all over small bodies. Kaiwaka said that god means good orderly direction but my brother told him that god means good onerous deeds and that you have to act god out. If you go looking for a sign that you're living right, you won't find one. It's doing living things that gives god a chance. Whatever he meant, it made sense to me. He said no one can hear you when you talk to yourself so it's no good praying with your eyes and mouth closed. You were very small, Aotahi. His wife will decide about whether the dog is a boy or a girl and whether it sleeps inside or out. Other people's brothers would've asked to see the sharp stick that Kaiwaka always talks about and if they were really bored they'd tell him to go on and do it then. My brother said that everything given is taken away in one go but that it returns to you over time. It's like swimming back to yourself from a great distance. Ruawahia is a star that marks the ninth month. My brother and Kaiwaka and the other children need to keep sharing stories and listening to each other. They are together apart, they are unrepeatable moments. My brother knows a lot about what you should do to keep yourself safe and what might get you hurt. Whatever Kaiwaka said to my brother I just smile through my tears. They dance in the same wide opus of darkness and suspended inferno. I have to remember to act out god with my eyes and mouth open.

He's going to name his children after constellations. Te Tira o Puanga is the light of Orion's belt. My brother helped Kaiwaka with his learning because Kaiwaka threatened to cut himself otherwise. They made a song about birds with lots of interesting facts. My brother was good at colouring in the blank space between words and people. Te Ikaroa is the Milky Way. They drew pictures of germs crawling all over small bodies. Kaiwaka said that god means good orderly direction but my brother told him that god means good onerous deeds and that you have to act god out. If you go looking for a sign that you're living right, you won't find one. It's doing living things that gives god a chance. Whatever he meant, it made sense to me. He said no one can hear you when you talk to yourself so it's no good praying with your eyes and mouth closed. You were very small, Aotahi. His wife will decide about whether the dog is a boy or a girl and whether it sleeps inside or out. Other people's brothers would've asked to see the sharp stick that Kaiwaka always talks about and if they were really bored they'd tell him to go on and do it then. My brother said that everything given is taken away in one go but that it returns to you over time. It's like swimming back to yourself from a great distance. Ruawahia is a star that marks the ninth month. My brother and Kaiwaka and the other children need to keep sharing stories and listening to each other. They are together apart, they are unrepeatable moments. My brother knows a lot about what you should do to keep yourself safe and what might get you hurt. I counted his fingers and toes, all of them soft and still. Whatever Kaiwaka said to my brother I just smile through my tears. They dance in the same wide opus of darkness and suspended inferno. I have to remember to act out god with my eyes and mouth open.

He's going to name his children after constellations. Te Tira o Puanga is the light of Orion's belt. My brother helped Kaiwaka with his learning because Kaiwaka threatened to cut himself otherwise. They made a song about birds with lots of interesting facts. My brother was good at colouring in the blank space between words and people. Te Ikaroa is the Milky Way. They drew pictures of germs crawling all over small bodies. Kaiwaka said that god means good orderly direction but my brother told him that god means good onerous deeds and that you have to act god out. If you go looking for a sign that you're living right, you won't find one. It's doing living things that gives god a chance. Whatever he meant, it made sense to me. He said no one can hear you when you talk to yourself so it's no good praying with your eyes and mouth closed. If you keep hoping for good things to happen all around you but you don't have time to open your eyes and greet a stranger, then my brother says you're missing out. You were very small, Aotahi. His wife will decide about whether the dog is a boy or a girl and whether it sleeps inside or out. Other people's brothers would've asked to see the sharp stick that Kaiwaka always talks about and if they were really bored they'd tell him to go on and do it then. My brother said that everything given is taken away in one go but that it returns to you over time. It's like swimming back to yourself from a great distance. His pearly skin could barely hold a heart. Ruawahia is a star that marks the ninth month. My brother and Kaiwaka and the other children need to keep sharing stories and listening to each other. They are together apart, they are unrepeatable moments. My brother knows a lot about what you should do to keep yourself safe and what might get you hurt. I counted his fingers and toes, all of them soft and still. Whatever Kaiwaka said to my brother I just smile through my tears. They dance in the same wide opus of darkness and suspended inferno. I have to remember to act out god with my eyes and mouth open.

He's going to name his children after constellations. Te Tira o Puanga is the light of Orion's belt. My brother helped Kaiwaka with his learning because Kaiwaka threatened to cut himself otherwise. They made a song about birds with lots of interesting facts. My brother was good at colouring in the blank space between words and people. Te Ikaroa is the Milky Way. They drew pictures of germs crawling all over small bodies. Kaiwaka said that god means good orderly direction but my brother told him that god means good onerous deeds and that you have to act god out. If you go looking for a sign that you're living right, you won't find one. It's doing living things that gives god a chance. Whatever he meant, it made sense to me. I trust my brother because he's really lived and that's when you know someone's done something truly godly. He said no one can hear you when you talk to yourself so it's no good praying with your eyes and mouth closed. If you keep hoping for good things to happen all around you but you don't have time to open your eyes and greet a stranger, then my brother says you're missing out. You were very small, Aotahi. His wife will decide about whether the dog is a boy or a girl and whether it sleeps inside or out. Other people's brothers would've asked to see the sharp stick that Kaiwaka always talks about and if they were really bored they'd tell him to go on and do it then. My brother said that everything given is taken away in one go but that it returns to you over time. It's like swimming back to yourself from a great distance. His pearly skin could barely hold a heart. Ruawahia is a star that marks the ninth month. My brother and Kaiwaka and the other children need to keep sharing stories and listening to each other. They are together apart, they are unrepeatable moments. My brother knows a lot about what you should do to keep yourself safe and what might get you hurt. I counted his fingers and toes, all of them soft and still. Whatever Kaiwaka said to my brother I just smile through my tears. They dance in the same wide opus of darkness and suspended inferno. Aotahi is made of all the people and words around space. I have to remember to act out god with my eyes and mouth open.

He's going to name his children after constellations. Te Tira o Puanga is the light of Orion's belt. My brother helped Kaiwaka with his learning because Kaiwaka threatened to cut himself otherwise. They made a song about birds with lots of interesting facts. My brother was good at colouring in the blank space between words and people. Te Ikaroa is the Milky Way. The other children liked the things they learned about cleanliness and godliness. They drew pictures of germs crawling all over small bodies. Kaiwaka said that god means good orderly direction but my brother told him that god means good onerous deeds and that you have to act god out. If you go looking for a sign that you're living right, you won't find one. It's doing living things that gives god a chance. Whatever he meant, it made sense to me. I trust my brother because he's really lived and that's when you know someone's done something truly godly. He said no one can hear you when you talk to yourself so it's no good praying with your eyes and mouth closed. If you keep hoping for good things to happen all around you but you don't have time to open your eyes and greet a stranger, then my brother says you're missing out. You were very small, Aotahi. His wife will decide about whether the dog is a boy or a girl and whether it sleeps inside or out. Other people's brothers would've asked to see the sharp stick that Kaiwaka always talks about and if they were really bored they'd tell him to go on and do it then. My brother said that everything given is taken away in one go but that it returns to you over time. It's like swimming back to yourself from a great distance. His pearly skin could barely hold a heart. Ruawahia is a star that marks the ninth month. My brother and Kaiwaka and the other children need to keep sharing stories and listening to each other. They are together apart, they are unrepeatable moments. My brother knows a lot about what you should do to keep yourself safe and what might get you hurt. I counted his fingers and toes, all of them soft and still. Aotahi is a tapu star that dwells alone. Whatever Kaiwaka said to my brother I just smile through my tears. They dance in the same wide opus of darkness and suspended inferno. Aotahi is made of all the people and words around space. I have to remember to act out god with my eyes and mouth open. I saw you, Aotahi, turn and rise.

43

He's going to name his children after constellations. Te Tira o Puanga is the light of Orion's belt. My brother helped Kaiwaka with his learning because Kaiwaka threatened to cut himself otherwise. They made a song about birds with lots of interesting facts. My brother was good at colouring in the blank space between words and people. Te Ikaroa is the Milky Way. The other children liked the things they learned about cleanliness and godliness. They drew pictures of germs crawling all over small bodies. Kaiwaka said that god means good orderly direction but my brother told him that god means good onerous deeds and that you have to act god out. If you go looking for a sign that you're living right, you won't find one. It's doing living things that gives god a chance. Whatever he meant, it made sense to me. I trust my brother because he's really lived and that's when you know someone's done something truly godly. He said no one can hear you when you talk to yourself so it's no good praying with your eyes and mouth closed. If you keep hoping for good things to happen all around you but you don't have time to open your eyes and greet a stranger, then my brother says you're missing out. You were very small, Aotahi. His wife will decide about whether the dog is a boy or a girl and whether it sleeps inside or out. Other people's brothers would've asked to see the sharp stick that Kaiwaka always talks about and if they were really bored they'd tell him to go on and do it then. My brother said that everything given is taken away in one go but that it returns to you over time. It's like swimming back to yourself from a great distance. His pearly skin could barely hold a heart. Ruawahia is a star that marks the ninth month. My brother and Kaiwaka and the other children need to keep sharing stories and listening to each other. They are together apart, they are unrepeatable moments. My brother knows a lot about what you should do to keep yourself safe and what might get you hurt. I counted his fingers and toes, all of them soft and still. Aotahi is a tapu star that dwells alone. Whatever Kaiwaka said to my brother I just smile through my tears. They dance in the same wide opus of darkness and suspended inferno. Aotahi is made of all the people and words around space. I have to remember to act out god with my eyes and mouth open. I saw you, Aotahi, turn and rise.

He's going to name his children after constellations. Te Tira o Puanga is the light of Orion's belt. My brother helped Kaiwaka with his learning because Kaiwaka threatened to cut himself otherwise. They made a song about birds with lots of interesting facts. My brother was good at colouring in the blank space between words and people. Te Ikaroa is the Milky Way. The other children liked the things they learned about cleanliness and godliness. They drew pictures of germs crawling all over small bodies. Kaiwaka said that god means good orderly direction but my brother told him that god means good onerous deeds and that you have to act god out. If you go looking for a sign that you're living right, you won't find one. It's doing living things that gives god a chance. Whatever he meant, it made sense to me. I trust my brother because he's really lived and that's when you know someone's done something truly godly. He said no one can hear you when you talk to yourself so it's no good praying with your eyes and mouth closed. If you keep hoping for good things to happen all around you but you don't have time to open your eyes and greet a stranger, then my brother says you're missing out. You were very small, Aotahi. His wife will decide about whether the dog is a boy or a girl and whether it sleeps inside or out. Other people's brothers would've asked to see the sharp stick that Kaiwaka always talks about and if they were really bored they'd tell him to go on and do it then. My brother said that everything given is taken away in one go but that it returns to you over time. It's like swimming back to yourself from a great distance. His pearly skin could barely hold a heart. Ruawahia is a star that marks the ninth month. My brother and Kaiwaka and the other children need to keep sharing stories and listening to each other. They are together apart, they are unrepeatable moments. My brother knows a lot about what you should do to keep yourself safe and what might get you hurt. I counted his fingers and toes, all of them soft and still. Aotahi is a tapu star that dwells alone. Whatever Kaiwaka said to my brother I just smile through my tears. They dance in the same wide opus of darkness and suspended inferno. Aotahi is made of all the people and words around space. I have to remember to act out god with my eyes and mouth open. I saw you, Aotahi, turn and rise.

THE COCONUT KING

The coconut king sends me a text
/ he wants to meet up and give me some coconut oil
/ it isn't cold pressed
/ his mother made it the traditional way in the sun
/ he's from a different island where the women are in charge
/ their men wait on them at home like wives in the west
/ Helena says it's fine to have a holiday fling
/ even if it's with the blackest guy on the island
/ my aunty says to keep away from him
/ he's a heart breaker
/ she should know
/ always getting caught on rusty men like rusty nails
/ smartening up in a blue floral dress
/ she puts on dangly earrings and does a twirl
/ pretty as a picture
/ I watch her leave the house smiling
/ promise not to see the black animal
/ lying through my teeth.

Helena's scooter works again
/ hear it turn into my aunty's drive
/ look down at myself in a pink mood singlet
/ blushing into red at the end
/ wipe passionfruit pulp off my shorts
/ stop in the mirror
/ turn my neck both ways
/ clean and slender
/ hair smelling like honey
/ skin soft like butter
/ take some deep breaths
/ watch the black ants march across the bench
/ Helena yells out over the spitting engine of the bike
/ hurry up and lock the house.

We get to the markets while it's still light
/ the coconut king is sitting in a circle with his boys
/ they fish and hunt together
/ bark at tourists in hotels
/ wearing next to nothing
/ stamp and wail about the gods

/ pull white women up from the audience to dance and dance
/ warriors for hire
/ call it round the world but it's just round the room
/ round and round the same island playing the same songs
every Tuesday and Thursday
/ he looks up
/ sees my face
/ jumps to his feet
/ tells the boys to shut up
/ does his best impression of a gentleman
/ pats down the black curls of his chest
/ creeping out from under his singlet
/ wades towards me
/ used to living underwater
/ wades through an ocean of women staring
/ saying dirty things behind his back
/ looks at me like I'm the only girl at the market
/ gives me a kiss on the cheek and two containers of white cake
/ Helena's eyes go wide
/ she grabs them out of my hands
/ stalks off to a table with shade
/ takes out her phone to text her papa'a boyfriend
/ snaps a picture of the cake
/ then a picture of her bust
/ gleaming behind a sunburst knot.

I walk around the food stalls with the coconut king
/ watch his leather skin glistening in the heat
/ beads of sweat push their way through his temples
/ I let him rest his fingers on my elbow
/ let him hold my hand for a second before my steak roll is ready
/ we walk to the back of the markets and cuddle by the toilets
/ he melts in my arms.

The church took my grandmother's stove
/ she signed the house over in her will
/ I go to the flat land where she used to live and feel all the
hairs on the back of my neck stand up
/ she was a quiet woman
/ always by the window lathering coconut oil into her hair

/ combing until the white teeth turned red
/ pleased when her scalp was raw
/ my aunty says not to think about it
/ the missionaries gave her something to believe in
/ we drive to a garden on the other side of the island to pick
frangipani for guests arriving from America
/ more old white men to line the pockets of the island
/ my aunty asks why I keep smiling
/ tell her the truth
/ I'm still drunk from the night before
/ when we get to the house there's only babies rolling around
on the deck and two dogs in chains
/ the mum and dad aren't home
/ we fill up a plastic bag with flowers and take off.

The darkest moments of the island unfurl in daylight
/ geckos cluck
/ fat with spirits
/ in the car we talk about moves
/ I want to inhabit his body
/ how to move inside the coconut king like water moves
inside the land
/ Helena talks me through her wardrobe
/ I can borrow whatever
/ I'm going home in three days anyway
/ her papa'a boyfriend thinks I can do better
/ someone with a brain
/ we smile at each other while my aunty drives
/ his blonde eyelashes shine
/ Helena's riding shotgun and making a long list
/ a shopping list
/ a beautification list
/ not that the coconut king will notice
/ my aunty's given up
/ I'm old enough
/ girls my age make up their own minds
/ their own beds
/ their own faces with clouds of powder.

Studying the coconut king one night drinking cheap vodka
/ dark and wide like a massive shadow with paws
/ after the vodka he kisses my hand and leads me down the
beach far away from Helena and her papa'a boyfriend
/ closer to the edge of trees and rocks
/ as clouds cover the moon
/ the coconut king takes off his shirt
/ lays it across the wet sand
/ he takes off his pants
/ kneels down on his crumpled clothes with both hands
reaching out to me
/ come and dance he says
/ the waves are playing our song.

Sheets on the line hold their breath
/ show off sharp ribs
/ hold hands breathe out
/ everything is moving on the island
/ old faces reappear
/ asking the same old questions
/ why did they send you away
/ were you a bad girl
/ is that why your tongue is a dead fish
/ did you kill your own tongue
/ spitting city trash
/ sitting unconscious in your own skin
/ far away from your people
/ sitting on the surface
/ is it like being covered in plastic
/ they ask over and over again
/ flicking their dusty tongues between English and gibberish.

Helena lies in the sun
/ waits for her glass to be filled
/ I pour pinot noir
/ her papa'a boyfriend has turned to gold
/ he sits down on the grass beside us
/ rolls a joint
/ they've got a cat who likes to fight
/ maybe they'll get married and stay on the rock

/ teach the cat to love the heat
/ Helena wants to study long distance
/ do it on the internet in town once a week
/ they've both gotten used to seeing the dead
/ things go on here
/ the elders are healing people by ending their lives
/ moving their souls into animals
/ that explains red-eyed roosters and goats looking for privacy
/ why the wild pigs cry like boys
/ they say that's what happened to my grandmother
/ the church swapped her for a dog
/ took all of her land
/ sold all of her jewels
/ Helena's papa'a boyfriend jokes about me and the coconut king
/ does he seem like a normal man
/ how can I not feel what he is
/ sleeping with a mountain ghost.

The coconut king turns up on his motorbike
/ I kiss Helena on the forehead
/ wave goodbye to her papa'a boyfriend
/ think about staying away for a while
/ send my aunty a text that I won't be home tonight
/ she replies with a smiley face.

We curve our way around the land
/ climbing high above the sea
/ pull up in front of a small house
/ he says it belongs to him
/ inside there's no electronics only coconut shells and soft fabrics
/ a single bed neatly made
/ boxes of beer and posters of wrestlers on the walls
/ I hitch up my long skirt
/ fan my face with a car magazine beside the bed.

The coconut king sits on the floor in front of me
/ rests his hands in his lap
/ goes soft around the mouth
/ everyone wants me to stay
/ goes soft around the eyes
/ tells me to cancel my flights
/ it's easy he knows the number
/ his brother will answer
/ my aunty will get a refund
/ I can stay with him on the mountain
/ my tongue won't be a dead fish
/ he knows where they've taken my grandmother's stove
/ we'll make them pay.

He says all of these things with the back of his head bleeding
handfuls and handfuls of blood
/ the room fills with small red waves
/ staining the heavy flowers of my long skirt.

TANIWHA HOUSE

IN HIS ROOM

The girl-woman's grandfather likes her to keep her nails clean.

'Keep your nails clean. People will think you come from a good-for-nothing family, if you step out of this house with dirty little, black little, muddy little nails!' Now he sits alone in his room inspecting his own nails for dirt. Humming songs long out of fashion, remembering to check his horses at the TAB and patting his pockets for the expectant chime of coins. It's security, isn't it? To know where you put things, the way they sound and the things they do. Coins don't move or get spent unless it's you doing the stuff. You do the stuff!

IN THE DEN

Her left breast in his right hand is a bit of an anticlimax. She knows, because he looks down at his own naked chest and contemplates the difference. If there is one it's minimal. Neither of them remark on how they appear to be reflections of the same design, how their bodies part and close in sequential formation dutifully, robotically. *She* keeps telling *him* to hush, but really there's no noise in the den except for the cat in the corner, Marcy, who keeps watching with sparkly eyes and clawing the carpet. She reminds the girl-woman of the devil. It's strange because she only met god recently, but already she's sure the two of them (god and the devil) are fighting over her soul like you would a toy with your pet sister, or so she imagines dramatically while the boy-man kisses her spine.

IN THE KITCHEN

From here she watches him fiddle with the clock and small
bits of brass in the dining room. Every now and then he
looks up with an open mouth and nods. It's strange to see
his mouth hang in the air like that. It's strange to imagine
that same hanging mouth on her naked skin come nightfall.
Surely!

In the oven, pork fat is crackling and everywhere around
her the smell of pork is becoming strangely (yes, strangely,
everything is strange to this woman today) arousing. The
cracked pepper in the mortar waffles up by the onions that
are next to the pantry on the far left side of the granite bench,
where the grain is at its most grainy.

She keeps asking him about the opera in town. 'Like
to go?' Or maybe a horse ride somewhere along one of the
West Coast beaches where women walk in sarongs with
unshaved legs.

IN HIS ROOM

Last night his wife visited him again. She does that when it's especially dark and she can hear the sound of his heart slowing, giving up and letting go. Every time it's a different guilt trip. She doesn't care that he's tired. She brings up old movies they used to watch and the way their daughter looked when she was first born – like a bird with a long beaky nose – and how they'd both laughed when they saw her, that hard-kind-of-guts laugh that only young people can do. That full-in-the-face laugh where you don't give a shit about your worries or the years on you because there's barely any! It's just life getting funny, and you're there in the crossroads saying to yourself, *Gee, how did I get to this impossible place? I love it! Tell me the way back? I have to know the way back – for always!*

IN THE DEN

Both are mystified by the infinity of skin... it stretches on over vein trails and sleepy eyes, it keeps touching itself, overheating - pulling away and changing in texture. She feels like a vessel of history and says so. Everything they do is so ancient, the words they whisper are straight out of films and cartoons and EVERYONE'S, EVERYONE'S saying the same, or they've said it already. She's lying like the woman from *Titanic*, or the pale women in the works of Rembrandt, or Beyoncé in one of her video clips. *He* thinks he can hear time and it isn't this: *tick tock tick tock* - it's the sound of his guides, ancestors, prophets and demons recounting in loud voices his birth and boyhood, his fears, and all the petty things a child desires and why he desires them still. Why now, so close, are the intimates released from love right at the curtain call of its performance?

IN THE KITCHEN

'Like to go?' He nods every time! But they go nowhere, and every bach she thinks of booking gets booked before she thinks to *really* book it, by some far more enthusiastic family who have time to drive through small creeks with their Land Rover and their brilliant, smiley children.

The girl-woman's father looks up from his work and thinks he sees a touch of Marilyn Monroe in the way his wife smiles. It's a statement, demanding nothing in return. It isn't expectant, like the facial exchanges between men that are designed to settle who is alpha and who is delta, who has the prettier wife and the more successful portfolio, who can afford bacon with their French toast girth-wise. No, no... not his wife!

She smiles like there's a camera looking back at her, but the camera has no film in it, and there's no photographer standing, excited, with a tripod and a fat cup of cream coffee.

IN HIS ROOM

The girl-woman's grandfather likes her to keep her nails clean.

'Keep your nails clean. People will think you come from a good-for-nothing family if you step out of this house with dirty little, black little, muddy little nails!' Now he sits alone in his room inspecting his own nails for dirt. Humming songs long out of fashion, remembering to check his horses at the TAB and patting his pockets for the expectant chime of coins. It's security, isn't it? To know where you put things, the way they sound and the things they do. Coins don't move or get spent unless it's you doing the stuff. You do the stuff!

IN THE DEN

Her left breast in his right hand is a bit of an anticlimax. She knows, because he looks down at his own naked chest and contemplates the difference. If there is one it's minimal. Neither of them remark on how they appear to be reflections of the same design, how their bodies part and close in sequential formation dutifully, robotically. *She* keeps telling *him* to hush, but really there's no noise in the den except for the cat in the corner, Marcy, who keeps watching with sparkly eyes and clawing the carpet. She reminds the girl-woman of the devil. It's strange because she only met god recently, but already she's sure the two of them (god and the devil) are fighting over her soul like you would a toy with your pet sister, or so she imagines dramatically while the boy-man kisses her spine.

IN THE KITCHEN

From here she watches him fiddle with the clock and small bits of brass in the dining room. Every now and then he looks up with an open mouth and nods. It's strange to see his mouth hang in the air like that. It's strange to imagine that same hanging mouth on her naked skin come nightfall. Surely!

In the oven, pork fat is crackling and everywhere around her the smell of pork is becoming strangely (yes, strangely, everything is strange to this woman today) arousing. The cracked pepper in the mortar waffles up by the onions that are next to the pantry on the far left side of the granite bench, where the grain is at its most grainy.

She keeps asking him about the opera in town. 'Like to go?' Or maybe a horse ride somewhere along one of the West Coast beaches where women walk in sarongs with unshaved legs.

IN HIS ROOM

Last night his wife visited him again. She does that when
it's especially dark and she can hear the sound of his heart
slowing, giving up and letting go. Every time it's a different
guilt trip. She doesn't care that he's tired. She brings up
old movies they used to watch and the way their daughter
looked when she was first born – like a bird with a long beaky
nose – and how they'd both laughed when they saw her, that
hard-kind-of-guts laugh that only young people can do. That
full-in-the-face laugh where you don't give a shit about your
worries or the years on you because there's barely any! It's just
life getting funny, and you're there in the crossroads saying
to yourself, *Gee, how did I get to this impossible place? I love
it! Tell me the way back? I have to know the way back – for
always!*

IN THE DEN

Both are mystified by the infinity of skin... it stretches
on over vein trails and sleepy eyes, it keeps touching itself,
overheating – pulling away and changing in texture. She feels
like a vessel of history and says so. Everything they do is so
ancient, the words they whisper are straight out of films and
cartoons and EVERYONE'S, EVERYONE'S saying the same,
or they've said it already. She's lying like the woman from
Titanic, or the pale women in the works of Rembrandt, or
Beyoncé in one of her video clips. *He* thinks he can hear time
and it isn't this: *tick tock tick tock* – it's the sound of his guides,
ancestors, prophets and demons recounting in loud voices his
birth and boyhood, his fears, and all the petty things a child
desires and why he desires them still. Why now, so close, are
the intimates released from love right at the curtain call of its
performance?

'Like to go?' He nods every time! But they go nowhere, and every bach she thinks of booking gets booked before she thinks to *really* book it, by some far more enthusiastic family who have time to drive through small creeks with their Land Rover and their brilliant, smiley children.

The girl-woman's father looks up from his work and thinks he sees a touch of Marilyn Monroe in the way his wife smiles. It's a statement, demanding nothing in return. It isn't expectant, like the facial exchanges between men that are designed to settle who is alpha and who is delta, who has the prettier wife and the more successful portfolio, who can afford bacon with their French toast girth-wise. No, no... not his wife!

She smiles like there's a camera looking back at her, but the camera has no film in it, and there's no photographer standing, excited, with a tripod and a fat cup of cream coffee.

IN HIS ROOM

When they were young he never forgot to love her – he wasn't one of those busy men short on time. He *made* time move around the both of them. That's what love is/was/ should be: the moving of time around people and things; the ability to stop the day in its tracks and kiss your sweetheart. Really *kiss* your sweetheart.

In the den, the girl-woman isn't much of a woman or a girl today... tonight. She's a bird more than anything, flying out of herself enough to see the lay of the land. It doesn't look the way she thought it would. She imagined some kind of rainbow fortress, maybe. An emerald empire, probably.

In the kitchen, the clock comes back to life.

IN THE DEN

By now he's kissed every single millimetre of her body and eaten everything she's cooked and spoken to her like this: love, lovely, lover and finally 'woman'. She lets him call her woman and they talk about what it means to freeze meat, why it keeps just as good and how more people should do it. Freshness is a thing of the past, she really agrees on that and so does he – they both nod. Yes, yes, freeze everything! Freshness is a thing of the past!

IN HIS ROOM

The girl-woman's grandfather likes her to keep her nails clean.

'Keep your nails clean. People will think you come from a good-for-nothing family if you step out of this house with dirty little, black little, muddy little nails!' Now he sits alone in his room inspecting his own nails for dirt. Humming songs long out of fashion, remembering to check his horses at the TAB and patting his pockets for the expectant chime of coins. It's security, isn't it? To know where you put things, the way they sound and the things they do. Coins don't move or get spent unless it's you doing the stuff. You do the stuff!

IN THE DEN

Her left breast in his right hand is a bit of an anticlimax. She knows, because he looks down at his own naked chest and contemplates the difference. If there is one it's minimal. Neither of them remark on how they appear to be reflections of the same design, how their bodies part and close in sequential formation dutifully, robotically. *She* keeps telling *him* to hush, but really there's no noise in the den except for the cat in the corner, Marcy, who keeps watching with sparkly eyes and clawing the carpet. She reminds the girl-woman of the devil. It's strange because she only met god recently, but already she's sure the two of them (god and the devil) are fighting over her soul like you would a toy with your pet sister, or so she imagines dramatically while the boy-man kisses her spine.

IN THE KITCHEN

From here she watches him fiddle with the clock and small bits of brass in the dining room. Every now and then he looks up with an open mouth and nods. It's strange to see his mouth hang in the air like that. It's strange to imagine that same hanging mouth on her naked skin come nightfall. Surely!

In the oven, pork fat is crackling and everywhere around her the smell of pork is becoming strangely (yes, strangely, everything is strange to this woman today) arousing. The cracked pepper in the mortar waffles up by the onions that are next to the pantry on the far left side of the granite bench, where the grain is at its most grainy.

She keeps asking him about the opera in town. 'Like to go?' Or maybe a horse ride somewhere along one of the West Coast beaches where women walk in sarongs with unshaved legs.

Last night his wife visited him again. She does that when it's especially dark and she can hear the sound of his heart slowing, giving up and letting go. Every time it's a different guilt trip. She doesn't care that he's tired. She brings up old movies they used to watch and the way their daughter looked when she was first born – like a bird with a long beaky nose – and how they'd both laughed when they saw her, that hard-kind-of-guts laugh that only young people can do. That full-in-the-face laugh where you don't give a shit about your worries or the years on you because there's barely any! It's just life getting funny, and you're there in the crossroads saying to yourself, *Gee, how did I get to this impossible place? I love it! Tell me the way back? I have to know the way back – for always!'*

Both are mystified by the infinity of skin... it stretches on over vein trails and sleepy eyes. It keeps touching itself, overheating – pulling away and changing in texture. She feels like a vessel of history and says so. Everything they do is so ancient, the words they whisper are straight out of films and cartoons and EVERYONE'S, EVERYONE'S saying the same, or they've said it already. She's lying like the woman from *Titanic*, or the pale women in the works of Rembrandt, or Beyoncé in one of her video clips. *He* thinks he can hear time and it isn't this: *tick tock tick tock* – it's the sound of his guides, ancestors, prophets and demons recounting in loud voices his birth and boyhood, his fears, and all the petty things a child desires and why he desires them still. Why now, so close, are the intimates released from love right at the curtain call of its performance?

IN THE KITCHEN

'Like to go?' He nods every time! But they go nowhere, and every bach she thinks of booking gets booked before she thinks to *really* book it, by some far more enthusiastic family who have time to drive through small creeks with their Land Rover and their brilliant, smiley children.

The girl-woman's father looks up from his work and thinks he sees a touch of Marilyn Monroe in the way his wife smiles. It's a statement, demanding nothing in return. It isn't expectant, like the facial exchanges between men that are designed to settle who is alpha and who is delta, who has the prettier wife and the more successful portfolio, who can afford bacon with their French toast girth-wise. No, no... not his wife!

She smiles like there's a camera looking back at her, but the camera has no film in it, and there's no photographer standing, excited, with a tripod and a fat cup of cream coffee.

IN HIS ROOM

When they were young he never forgot to love her – he wasn't one of those busy men short on time. He *made* time move around the both of them. That's what love is/was/ should be: the moving of time around people and things; the ability to stop the day in its tracks and kiss your sweetheart. Really *kiss* your sweetheart.

IN THE DEN

The girl-woman isn't much of a woman or a girl today... tonight. She's a bird more than anything, flying out of herself enough to see the lay of the land. It doesn't look the way she thought it would. She imagined some kind of rainbow fortress, maybe. An emerald empire, probably.

IN THE KITCHEN

The clock comes back to life.

MANIFESTO

'Thank God that's over...'

'For fuck's sake, what a talkfest!'

'I wish they'd put some chairs out.'

'My feet hurt.'

'My brain hurts!'

'He kept looking at me right in the eyes.
My cheeks are so sore from smiling! Oh,
"researching in the south of France," and,
"getting a kick out of street food in Brazil,"
ladidadida... I wanted to claw out his eyes
when he started wanking on and on about
his muse.'

'And it was his dog? I mean, I was surprised,
especially since he left it here. In a kennel with
strangers while he took off to New York? What
an absolute arse!'

'For three months too. We should report him to
the SPCA or something.'

'Why do we come to these wretched things?'

'For the wine? To be seen to be "active",
darling! You still writing?'

'Yeah, my ideals keep me warm at night, not
the pittance I'm living off. Can't afford leather,
heels, almond milk – the basic necessities of life.'

'Living the dream then?'

'Oh, absolutely, that puts some shine on the
struggle. Still painting?'

'I've moved into design.'

'Sick of starving, Ben?'

'You said it, sister. Did you actually understand
his manifesto rant?'

'Fuck, no, it flew right over my head!'

'Does Professor Moneybags expect anyone to
follow this, like some kind of cult? I mean, look
at this shit! *"1. Creativity is the hospital within
which craft is born. 2. Unfurl as the native fern
seeks sanctuary in its own intricacies. 3. You
are either artist or market, there is nothing in
between."* How is he allowed out in public?'

'Art is such a church, but without any paradise
beyond the grave.'

'My feet are on fire. I wish they'd come around
with the wine.'

'It's so hot up here, full of curling antipasti,
more dip than bread.'

'Why do they do that? It's like they've declared
war on focaccia.'

'Yeah, sorry, you're all... struggling, poor
dears...'

'We love artists, especially young artists.'

'*Especially* brown *young artists.*'

'Oh, yes, young Maori and Pasifika artists, we
love you!'

'We just don't want to feed you.'

'No, we'd like to drown you in pesto—'

'Tapenade, ha!'

'Chalk-like cheese sticks.'

'Bloody red merlot!'

'For a tummy ache.'

'Speeches by zombies.'

'Rich, fat old men.'

'For a hand job!'

'And money, promises like mist!'

'For heartache, I mean. But we love young
artists, truly...'

'We just want you to kill each other!'

'With your sharp ideas!'

'Your desperate edginess...'

'So edgy your prints could cut a man!'

'So edgy, there's no middle!'

'God, I love you, Ben, you're such a queen.'

'Most people can't keep up with my raving, but you – well, you're a different breed altogether, Caro.'

'You're making me blush! Busy week?'

'Just the usual, darling. Funding rounds more like fuck-off rounds!'

'Miss out?'

'Yes, and last time... every bloody time.'

'It's exactly like those last-girl-standing narratives.'

'I volunteer as Contribute!'

'What's that?'

'That's what my weapon would be... the power to collaborate!'

'Wow, Ben, you could've written that crazy manifesto!'

'That "manifesto" is more like a to-do list for the rich – so, no, not with these empty pockets, my dear. Are you still seeing what's-his-face? I met him last month, didn't I?'

'Tane... yep. We're going through a bit of a rough patch. You met him at the Black Pen Portraits.'

'Yeah, that's right. He seemed like a nice enough guy.'

'He was in Auckland for his sister's birthday. I'm kind of pleased he's not here tonight.'

'Why? What's up?'

'I think it's the age thing. He's almost as old as my dad...'

'Sounds promising so far.'

'And I think he's seeing someone else...'

'Well, you aren't exclusive, are you? Do you want to be?'

'I don't know. He's not really into monogamy
he thinks it's anti-life, seeing as we're all
animals.'

        'Okay, I'm following, a bit new-age but I can
        kind of see his convenient twist on reality,
        darling.'

'I guess what really stings is that he doesn't *get*
my work. I send him links to various articles
but he refuses to read them...'

        'Freedom, honey, it's very modern, very "now."
        He just wants to know you as Caro the person,
        not Caro the persona!'

'It's a bit hard seeing someone who lives in a
different city.'

        'We all have our crosses to bear.'

'And it gets a bit shit paying for everything
when we do have time together. Tane is really
antiestablishment so he doesn't like to stay in
one job too long.'

        'Bit of a revolutionary, eh? Oh, Caro, you can
        work with that, can't you, honey – I mean,
        there's obviously a lot of potential there?'

'Plus he's still figuring out his sexuality and his
iwi, and whether or not he wants to commit.'

        'Sweetheart, it sounds ideal, all care and no

responsibility! Are you looking for a partner or
a prisoner? Time to drag your ass into the 21st
century!'

'Mum says I'm pursuing a very rich karmic life.'

        'It's all Netflix and green tea at my place. I
        mean, avoid it, whatever it is Pita and I have –
        it's pretty boring, babe.'

'Love is supposed to be boring! I want a
"markets on Sunday" kind of guy.'

        'Trust me, you don't. The grass is greener on
        the other side.'

'Someone solid, who could afford nice things
– like this huge manifesto brick. Listen to this:
"Klein folds the corners of the art universe into
a devilishly accessible origami swan." What the
fuck?'

        'I still don't get it.'

'Are we really stupid or is it that whole
Emperor's New Clothes thing? I understand
that we've kind of pledged ourselves to art—'

        'Like gangsters?'

'Kind of, I guess. And we're in this intangible
space.'

        'The space between, Caro?'

'Yes, Ben.'

                                                    'Noted!'

'But even "in between" there have to be things
to hold onto, right?'

                    'Honestly, I reckon Professor Klein is just keen
                    to renovate his kitchen or his second bathroom
                    and that's what this whole fucking book launch
                    is about. The thing is, most people, even
                    cynical little shits like us – *especially* people
                    like us – want to be surrounded by beautiful
                    and mysterious objects.'

'See, that's my problem with Tane!'

                            'And that's my problem with Persian rugs!'

'When will I get my shit together?'

                    'It's overrated, Caro. You get involved with
                    a silver fox, pay off your debts because he
                    covers the rent of course, and then as soon as
                    you're done with your student loan you go
                    and do something stupid like a Contiki tour
                    across Europe with friends; only they aren't
                    your friends, they're just dirty bastards from
                    your shitty office who want to visit sex clubs in
                    Amsterdam!'

'What? Sex clubs like – strangers going at it
right in front of you?'

'It was like watching a walrus trying to board a moving tram. Trust me, you don't wanna know.'

'You're nuts but I love you.'

'Aw, I love you too, babe, even though you're super uptight.'

'Are you going to flick Pita?'

'God, no. I said I was bored, honey, not dead! And life-as-we-know-it-Tim?'

'It's Tane. You're such a shit, Ben. And no – not until I've figured out how I feel.'

'We're doomed.'

'At least we don't have dogs for muses.'

'And we don't skimp on the bread!'

'If this is all there is... we've done reasonably well.'

'For now, my sweet.'

'There is only now.'

Today in Otara, walking to the sushi shop on the corner, I see my father disappear into a dairy.

He emerges moments later with a packet of cigarettes and a bottle of Coca Cola, I watch him walk to the one of the benches where the old men count their coins before heading into the TAB. He sits down with his gut hanging over bright board shorts. The beard he fought off while I was a girl has grown into a thick, unruly bush. Something glints – a silver sleeper in his right ear?

I've never seen my father in South Auckland, sitting among our people as though he belongs inside his skin. He lights a cigarette and starts to drink the Coca Cola with both legs bouncing. My father doesn't smoke and he detests sugary drinks. Once, when my sister came home with a bottle of lemonade, he threw her across the living room and then quietly made his way to the kitchen where he poured the entire contents down the drain.

My father doesn't like to go beyond the safety of the CBD because he thinks 'young punks' will steal his car or mug him for his shoes, or pick his pockets while he's walking through the markets. So he stays within the city and colours himself lighter and lighter with words like 'evolved' and 'modern' and 'self-made'. One day he is so light I pass him on the street and only realise it's him by the cloud of Old Spice that lingers long after he's gone.

My father doesn't talk about his village. I've never seen him wear a crown of flowers, or slap his hands in ecstasy to the sound of beating drums. But here he is sitting in a plume of smoke, chatting to a man covered in tatau and – remarkably – showing his own tattoo. From where I'm standing it looks like an armband with intricate details that I want to see up close. We were taught to pity people with tattoos; my father said they were making life very hard for themselves and that they couldn't expect to find good jobs. I have the Southern Cross glittering down my back.

My father gets up and shakes hands with all the men who have formed a tight circle around him, his packet of cigarettes divided up between the group. They're stunned by his generosity and so am I. He continues along the footpath, smiling at children who are wagging school in their uniforms, patting the smallest boy on the head. When I wagged during high school he set my mattress on fire in the backyard and I slept on the floor for months, wondering if he would ever speak to me again.

My father stops to give his spare change to an old woman rocking back and forth on a stack of dirty cardboard. She looks up at him with pleading eyes. I'm surprised when he crouches down in front of her and offers his ear. She leans forward and whispers something that makes him reach out and touch her forehead like a new age priest. There's a theory that Jesus was a Reiki master; maybe my father has had a midlife crisis and decided that he too wants to heal people with his bare hands, the same hands that snapped the neck of our pet rabbit when it was time for her to become a stew. I refused to eat dinner that night. My father said the rabbit was never my friend and that she was always going to end up in the pot – from the moment she was born the pot was waiting for her. He swore that there was a pot waiting for me too, big enough to hide my whole body and drown out my screams. It was supposed to be a metaphor about the cycle of life, to create a hardness in me not to trust anyone. For months afterwards I had nightmares that I was being boiled alive and seasoned by a giant hand.

I begin to doubt whether it really is my father, the man who refused to help me click-in my seat belt or open the lids of chilly bins or run a hot bath, which meant that I sat in cold water most nights. I follow him at a distance, watching his smart green polo entering the town square; he dips in and out of several shops, befriending shopkeepers and elders. In the last shop he takes an especially long time. I lean against the glass of the art gallery and pretend to check my phone. When he comes back out into the square my father is wearing a white floral shirt and a dark blue pareu. I wonder where his board shorts and polo shirt have gone, where he's parked his vintage car and if he's worried that it will be stolen.

There's an old woman waiting for him by the concrete stage in the square. She holds her arms out and he walks into them like a child coming home to his mother. She begins to speak to him in the language of his homeland and surprisingly he responds fluently, his tongue flicking each syllable away from him, the way my nana used to speak when she was alive. They hold hands as they finish their conversation. His face is soft and glistening with tears. It can't be my father. Maybe my grandparents were overwhelmed by twins, and they gave my uncle away to a kind family in Otara.

The drummers pass me, cackling, and beaming with huge smiles. They drag on their smokes and do up the last few buttons of their shirts, white like my father's, with fresh-flower eis around their necks. Behind them trail their sons carrying the drums and stands, sticks and cuts of fabric. They start setting themselves up and a small crowd gathers in front of the stage.

I look back to the spot where my father was and he's gone. There's no one there. Exactly like the absence he's occupied inside of me all these years. Maybe I feel relief to be let down again, to rest in the comfort that, no – he hasn't changed. I turn to go back to work, looking down at my phone and realising that my lecture starts in half an hour. I think about my students and how much I can't wait to see all of them and hear what they've been up to over the holidays. I stop outside the dairy where my father first appeared and dig around inside my handbag trying to find my car keys. I've given up on getting sushi.

Walking towards my car, I feel the air around me sour and sweeten. The walls of my family home close in. I can see the dark living room and the bottle-green couch where my mother drank herself to death. It's a scent conflicted between Old Spice and... coconut oil? The proper stuff that my nana used to comb through my hair, talking over my head in shark-bone raps, illuminating a strange ocean that I could never drink into my skin.

I turn around and see my father standing behind me in the car park, holding a crown of flowers in his hands. He reaches out and gently places the ei on my head. I can smell frangipani and tiare; I can see the gardens that my nana yearned for.

All the rage I've been holding onto steams up behind my eyes; the back of my throat feels like it's been dragged through broken glass.

He scoops me up into his arms as the drums begin their call. I bury my face in the blossoms of his floral shirt. I want to kill him, I want to peel the skin from his bones and find all the black holes.

I was proactive. I read a lot of books.

I watched *EastEnders* and my figure. If an idea broke the afternoon, off you went and that was fine.

There was a long road from our cottage to the pub. I walked there a hundred times, sometimes stopping to buy raw chicken wrapped in blood and gold. Sometimes a market appeared out of thin air and the villagers all had things to sell. Hell was well priced; for the cost of organic grapes you could buy *two* hells instead.

One we imagined together, bodies well lit in the Surrey sun – tending to a dead allotment, sinking our sweat into the soil.

The second hell came free. The kind I felt at night stacking the pots back in the wrong order, starting over a hundred times, hating the induction stove. All progress, all lies.

The staff at the pub were friendly but forgettable. I sat by myself and ordered huge meals. Beer-battered tears with a bucket of tartar. Rosewater pudding and pints of self-loathing.

The long winter made the footpaths slick. I twisted my ankle, I fell on my face.

You had driving lessons and spent most days discovering the English countryside. According to your silence, it was beautiful.

When spring came, the horrible fields transformed. I walked on my sprain to an apple tree. They were small and green with secret marks: some fallen and chipped, some too high for my hands. I left them all to their lives.

The curtains cried, the blue rug sat by the door in a ball. I would clear your plate and watch out of all the windows, bits of sky around the house and small stuff happening.

I know most of the cans have expired, especially the lentils in brine – why you'd want curried chickpeas and sardines in light oil I'll never know.

Ava answers *Yes*, turns on her heel and pauses... was it milk and *one* sugar or two? The pit bulls are barking next door; the sound of their heads butting against the fence distracts her for a while. It was definitely one sugar, she decides, making an executive decision encouraged by the elders staring down at her from the living room wall. Their faces share the same forced smile, a show of defiance masking years of hard work. Funny, she thinks, that one day she too will be a head on the wall, like a hunter's trophy complete with shell necklace, and ula fala for the talking chiefs, draped across a smiling, wordless mouth.

The uncles walk past carrying trays of beer, and somewhere in there she knows will be a deck of playing cards. Ava darts around them, forgetting the sound of dogs snapping at the air. On the way into the kitchen she walks through a cluster of bubbles pop, pop, pop they disappear into her hips, the kids in the hallway crying out.

What did Uncle Pat ask for again? A black tea with two sugars? He used to drink coffee with cream before the stroke and falling in love with another man... God. Ava decides he probably takes it black with one; the thought of sin makes her leave out the sugar altogether.

Mama – Ava's grandmother – asks her to fetch serving spoons, the good ones, long and white like swans. They're in the wooden-veneer china cabinet, resting inside a glass bowl. Beside it stand gold-lipped beer glasses and wine goblets; Mama tells anyone who will listen that she's saving them for the right occasion. At the bottom of the cabinet sit two stacks of blue china plates alongside a crystal vase from Aunty Penina, who bought it during a visit to Greece. All of Mama's nice things are taken out once a month to wipe away the dust. Ava will travel to where Aunty Penina bought the vase, she says over and over in her mind; she'll lie on the hot white sand with crystal blue waters all around, sipping one of those drinks that have an umbrella and cherries perched on the rim. Aunty Penina said it was just like visiting a postcard.

A tapa-framed picture of Pa leans back on the top shelf of

the cabinet. He smiles in black and white. Everyone pauses in front of his portrait as though they have uncovered a long-hidden treasure. They search for themselves in his features, trying to work out if they have his dark eyes. Ava remembers Pa, how he lived far away in the distance, and when the others sigh how special he was – how he kept the family together – she responds with the same forced smile.

Mama tells Ava to cut up the cakes. She sets aside a piece of lemon meringue pie for Mama's favourite son, Jack, who's coming late after training. Lou – Aunty Louisa, who demands everyone just call her Lou – calls out for a clean glass because a fat fly has landed in her juice. Lou laughs as the wet wings try to climb out.

Ava whimpers, her eyes fixated on the struggle for life. She calls *Yes* absentmindedly to her grandmother, pulls the juice out of the fridge and pours Lou another glass. She presses down on the button for the jug to boil, pulls cups from the pantry and levers the edge of a butter knife around the top of a coffee can. Footsteps crunch down the back footpath with more family walking towards the house. She can see them from the kitchen window and in her mind she assembles them into a steady stream of orders: 'Black with one, white with two, hot water with a slice of lemon, white with three...'

Prince comes over. He demands a Sprite and so do the rest of the boys standing in the driveway, leaning against one of the uncle's vans, trying to look cool. A couple of the older ones have promised Prince that they'll drive all the cousins down to the mall to look at the latest kicks and maybe have lunch there as well. 'Butter chicken curry,' Prince announces. Ava smiles and gives him the Sprite with a few plastic cups balanced upside down on top of the bottle. He runs off, eager to please. She knows they aren't going anywhere – none of those boys can drive.

The older cousins walk in, backs straight, hair coiffed delicately into place, bringing in the scent of lilies. Their fat-necked husbands look like the dogs next door. They're noisy without saying anything, practising for old age with grunts and coughs. One of them walks into the kitchen and Ava has to press hard against the sink to leave room for him so he can put his cans into the fridge. He turns around as if he's only just noticed her, 'You drink, little girl?' He leaves the kitchen laughing, his huge feet smacking against his jandals.

Ava walks around the edges, careful not to meet anyone's gaze, pretending to fuss with one of her cousins or tap at the screen of her phone, answering texts. Placing hot drinks in familiar hands, she replies to their smiling faces that yes, her big sister Lucia is doing well, and that no, Lucia doesn't have exams but she will soon, and nodding what a good thing it is that Ava isn't going anywhere – lucky that she can stick around and help the family. They have plans for her to take care of Mama after she finishes high school, or maybe her mother will return from Brisbane and take Ava back to God's waiting room where she can get a cleaning job in a good hotel. Aunty Lou offered to take her in but Mama shook her head; everyone knows that Lou drinks too much and beats her sons. Aunty Lou's husband ran off with a younger woman. She walks around mourning him incorrectly, like a fallen soldier who died for his country.

When Lucia and Ava talk on the phone Ava holds back tears and reminds her sister to ask questions if she doesn't understand something in her lectures; she tells Lucia that she's enjoying school but having a hard time accepting her place in the family. If only their mother would come home, then everything could go back to normal and the family would forgive her for all of the shame that follows her and her children and siblings and Mama around like a terrible plague. Only Lucia has escaped the plague and fought her way from the bottom of the food chain all the way to the top. Lucia sends Ava money in the mail, Australian tens and twenties, bright and plastic the way Ava imagines all of Sydney must be. She wants to see the candy city for herself and lie in Hyde Park where Lucia goes with her friends after uni to eat fish burgers and watch bats flying through the sky like paper darts.

Underneath Ava's bed there's a small chest with a lock where she keeps her money, plus a bucket list of all the things she wants to do before she dies. A lot of her friends have hung themselves in their own backyards, in rugby rooms and at the backs of churches where they've kneeled all their lives. People log onto Facebook and write messages to the youthful dead as though they've all gone apple picking down south, or stolen away on ships to find their fortunes in strange lands: 'Hey uce, hey bro, hey you still owe me a mince pie, you skux!' 'Guuurrrlll, I missed you SO MUCH today! School was dry!'

After Lucia flew to Sydney, Ava moped away into her bedroom and found an old gym bag with a long strap like a belt. She positioned the bag over her closet door with the strap hanging down, and then she put her head into the makeshift noose and let her whole body go. The bag broke, cheap and old as it was. Sitting in a heap on the floor, she decided to live, and the next day she made her bucket list.

When the old people fall asleep at night, Ava crawls out of her bed and holds her breath walking down the creaky hallway into the living room. She shuts the door behind her and turns the lights on, undoing her long plait, letting her midnight curls breathe. She sneaks a swig of gin from the bottle hidden in the pantry behind the soup bowls and then it's time to write songs that she can practice at school with her friends. It depends on her mood; some nights the songs are like just like hits you'd hear on the radio, all about love and calling someone when you say you will. On other nights the songs she writes are about animals: wolves and reindeer, or pandas eating bamboo. She never knows where the words will go, but every time she stops to imagine a world of colour and verse she feels a tinge of happiness that makes her think perhaps there's even more of that feeling inside of her – just behind the pain that's blocking her heart.

It grows darker, the men start to sing in the backyard, the cackling of the aunties dies down, the house feels still as Ava puts the leftovers away in the fridge. She feels a wet mouth on her knee – it's Kuli, black and wheezing, wanting a feed.

'Good dog, good devil,' Ava says, patting Kuli's dreaded face, taking all the bones from the pots and throwing them out of the window above the sink. The dog waddles off to find her feast in the weeds.

Eventually he comes back, the tree-trunk husband with a pit bull face. He pulls his rums out of the fridge and hands her a can – telling her to drink. Ava says, *Yes,* and puts it down beside the chopping board, making it look like she will. He turns around to see if anyone is coming and reaches out with both hands, massaging her new breasts as though he's done it a hundred times before. All the hairs on Ava's arms stand up. Without thinking, she grabs a knife that's drying beside the sink, still wet with bubbles, and thrusts it out in front of her, watching the dog husband lose his balance. The small of his back connects with the hard edge of the bench, Ava's wild eyes look down at the cans of rum he's dropped, spraying Cola froth across the lino, giving the tiny kitchen a fiesta feel. Then he's gone, back into the dark. Her eyes sting, the moon swings across the lawn.

The aunties come in and move around her, pulling the oven open, wetting cloths, filling the sink with hot soapy water, mopping the rum from the floor, muttering that it's a shame so-and-so got drunk and made a mess. 'Typical,' they all say. One pair of hands asks about Lucia, studying to become a doctor – Lucia, who's probably reading her textbooks right now.

'Did you know, Ava, your sister is the first in the family to ever go to university and the first to live away from home all by herself? That makes her a double achiever! I can't believe she's going to be a doctor! You must be so proud of her.'

Ava says, *Yes,* and goes to check on the washing. She wades through a sea of tiny limbs beside the washing line, parting around her like the Red Sea. The towels and table cloths are still damp, she fusses with the pegs and wipes down the table by the barbecue. There's a pool of sticky ice cream at the edge of the carport, pink and blue swirls that Kuli will discover after she's finished with her bones.

Ava walks through the back door and into the living room, stopping in front of the ghostly elders with Pa's eyes burning into the back of her head. She takes an ula fala down from one of the portraits and puts it around her neck, before walking through the long hallway and out the front door to sit on the porch alone.

Nobody comes to bring her a piece of cake or a bread roll, no one asks her how many sugars she wants in her tea. It doesn't matter, it's never mattered. She can hear the women looking for her but it's like they're under water, far away. The electric light buzzes beside the front door; lots of small insects are flying to their deaths, unable to resist the glow. Ava stands on the top step and unfolds her bucket list in the moonlight.

I will graduate with a degree in music... I will visit Greece...
I will feel the sun on my face at Hyde Park with Lucia...

You can
motivate millennial employees by putting pictures of cute
cats around the office.

We're going to have lunch at the fish markets near my work.

I walk
out of the stained-glass front door, headed for the bus stop.

In an unfair world, only the young and rich can thrive.

After dressing I walk around leisurely, deciding on shoes and earrings – there are so many nice things glittering in my jewellery box.

You can motivate millennial employees by putting pictures of cute cats around the office.

See Kate Middleton's exciting new look.

We're going to have lunch at the fish markets near my work.

I walk out of the stained-glass front door, headed for the bus stop.

This sticky lemon chicken is the perfect dinner party dish.

A NEW GEOLOGICAL STUDY MAY EXPLAIN HOW HAWAI'I
WAS FORMED.

In an unfair
world, only the young and rich can thrive.

HUNGARY ACCUSES MIGRANT PROTESTORS OF
TERRORISM FOR CLASHING WITH POLICE.

After dressing I walk around leisurely, deciding
on shoes and earrings – there are so many nice things glittering
in my jewellery box. POPE FRANCIS HEADS TO CUBA.

You can
motivate millennial employees by putting pictures of cute
cats around the office.

SEE KATE MIDDLETON'S EXCITING NEW LOOK.

We're going to have lunch at the fish markets near my work.
I put my dishes into
the kitchen sink and fill up my thermos with fresh ginger
tea.
I walk
out of the stained-glass front door, headed for the bus stop.

This sticky lemon chicken is the
perfect dinner party dish.

Does Xi Jinping care what America thinks of China?

A NEW GEOLOGICAL STUDY MAY EXPLAIN HOW HAWAI'I WAS FORMED.
ISRAELI AIRCRAFT HIT TARGETS IN GAZA AFTER ROCKETS ARE FIRED ON A TOWN. In an unfair world, only the young and rich can thrive.

HUNGARY ACCUSES MIGRANT PROTESTORS OF TERRORISM FOR CLASHING WITH POLICE.

After dressing I walk around leisurely, deciding on shoes and earrings – there are so many nice things glittering in my jewellery box. POPE FRANCIS HEADS TO CUBA.

You can motivate millennial employees by putting pictures of cute cats around the office.

SEE KATE MIDDLETON'S EXCITING NEW LOOK.

Arranged marriages don't always work for animals in captivity. We're going to have lunch at the fish markets near my work.
I put my dishes into the kitchen sink and fill up my thermos with fresh ginger tea.
I walk out of the stained-glass front door, headed for the bus stop.

This sticky lemon chicken is the perfect dinner party dish.
In a dream last night, two lions slept on either side of me while I sunbathed in the middle of the road.

Does Xi Jinping care what America thinks of China? After brushing my teeth, I wash my face with Clean & Clear Morning Burst. A NEW GEOLOGICAL STUDY MAY EXPLAIN HOW HAWAI'I WAS FORMED.

ISRAELI AIRCRAFT HIT TARGETS IN GAZA AFTER ROCKETS ARE FIRED ON A TOWN. In an unfair world, only the young and rich can thrive.

HUNGARY ACCUSES MIGRANT PROTESTORS OF TERRORISM FOR CLASHING WITH POLICE.

After dressing I walk around leisurely, deciding on shoes and earrings - there are so many nice things glittering in my jewellery box. POPE FRANCIS HEADS TO CUBA.

You can motivate millennial employees by putting pictures of cute cats around the office.

SEE KATE MIDDLETON'S EXCITING NEW LOOK.

Arranged marriages don't always work for animals in captivity. We're going to have lunch at the fish markets near my work. I put my dishes into the kitchen sink and fill up my thermos with fresh ginger tea.

I walk out of the stained-glass front door, headed for the bus stop. DEBRIS FOUND AT THE BOTTOM OF THE SEABED IS BELIEVED TO BE ATLANTIS.

This sticky lemon chicken is the perfect dinner party dish. I don't want to wait for another bus. HENRI MATISSE WAS BORN ON THIS DAY IN 1869. In a dream last night, two lions slept on either side of me while I sunbathed in the middle of the road.

I have an Oral-B electric toothbrush; I'm convinced it gives my teeth a superior clean. Does Xi Jinping care what America thinks of China? After brushing my teeth, I wash my face with Clean & Clear Morning Burst. A NEW GEOLOGICAL STUDY MAY EXPLAIN HOW HAWAI'I WAS FORMED.

ISRAELI AIRCRAFT HIT TARGETS IN GAZA AFTER ROCKETS ARE FIRED ON A TOWN. In an unfair world, only the young and rich can thrive. I pull out the top drawer and try to find my favourite aqua bra, a gift to myself last Christmas. HUNGARY ACCUSES MIGRANT PROTESTORS OF TERRORISM FOR CLASHING WITH POLICE. This chair is the result of years of research and experimentation; it intersects between art and science. After dressing I walk around leisurely, deciding on shoes and earrings – there are so many nice things glittering in my jewellery box. POPE FRANCIS HEADS TO CUBA.

You can motivate millennial employees by putting pictures of cute cats around the office. There is a full day of meetings ahead; I reply to five emails while eating half a cup of muesli with a cut-up pear. SEE KATE MIDDLETON'S EXCITING NEW LOOK.

Arranged marriages don't always work for animals in captivity. We're going to have lunch at the fish markets near my work. I put my dishes into the kitchen sink and fill up my thermos with fresh ginger tea.
Watch this spider turn wasps into mummified cowboys. I walk out of the stained-glass front door, headed for the bus stop. DEBRIS FOUND AT THE BOTTOM OF THE SEABED IS BELIEVED TO BE ATLANTIS.

This sticky lemon chicken is the perfect dinner party dish. I don't want to wait for another bus. HENRI MATISSE WAS BORN ON THIS DAY IN 1869. In a dream last night, two lions slept on either side of me while I sunbathed in the middle of the road. NIGERIAN PRESIDENT GATHERS SOLID EVIDENCE OF OIL CORRUPTION.

WHISTLEBLOWER EDWARD SNOWDEN TALKS ALIEN ENCRYPTION. I have an Oral-B electric toothbrush; I'm convinced it gives my teeth a superior clean. Does Xi Jinping care what America thinks of China? After brushing my teeth, I wash my face with Clean & Clear Morning Burst. A NEW GEOLOGICAL STUDY MAY EXPLAIN HOW HAWAI'I WAS FORMED. I like the tiny orange beads and how the face-wash builds into a gentle foam. ISRAELI AIRCRAFT HIT TARGETS IN GAZA AFTER ROCKETS ARE FIRED ON A TOWN. In an unfair world, only the young and rich can thrive. I pull out the top drawer and try to find my favourite aqua bra, a gift to myself last Christmas. HUNGARY ACCUSES MIGRANT PROTESTORS OF TERRORISM FOR CLASHING WITH POLICE. This chair is the result of years of research and experimentation; it intersects between art and science. After dressing I walk around leisurely, deciding on shoes and earrings – there are so many nice things glittering in my jewellery box. POPE FRANCIS HEADS TO CUBA.

You can motivate millennial employees by putting pictures of cute cats around the office. There is a full day of meetings ahead; I reply to five emails while eating half a cup of muesli with a cut-up pear. SEE KATE MIDDLETON'S EXCITING NEW LOOK.

Arranged marriages don't always work for animals in captivity. We're going to have lunch at the fish markets near my work. Why do women love to read about love? I put my dishes into the kitchen sink and fill up my thermos with fresh ginger tea. TIPS ON HOW TO PARENT WHEN YOU'RE BROKEN-HEARTED. Watch this spider turn wasps into mummified cowboys. I walk out of the stained-glass front door, headed for the bus stop. DEBRIS FOUND AT THE BOTTOM OF THE SEABED IS BELIEVED TO BE ATLANTIS.

This sticky lemon chicken is the perfect dinner party dish. I don't want to wait for another bus. HENRI MATISSE WAS BORN ON THIS DAY IN 1869. In a dream last night, two lions slept on either side of me while I sunbathed in the middle of the road. NIGERIAN PRESIDENT GATHERS SOLID EVIDENCE OF OIL CORRUPTION.

WHISTLEBLOWER EDWARD SNOWDEN TALKS ALIEN ENCRYPTION. What is cry editing in music videos? I have an Oral-B electric toothbrush; I'm convinced it gives my teeth a superior clean. Does Xi Jinping care what America thinks of China? After brushing my teeth, I wash my face with Clean & Clear Morning Burst. A NEW GEOLOGICAL STUDY MAY EXPLAIN HOW HAWAI'I WAS FORMED. I like the tiny orange beads and how the face-wash builds into a gentle foam. ISRAELI AIRCRAFT HIT TARGETS IN GAZA AFTER ROCKETS ARE FIRED ON A TOWN. In an unfair world, only the young and rich can thrive. I pull out the top drawer and try to find my favourite aqua bra, a gift to myself last Christmas. HUNGARY ACCUSES MIGRANT PROTESTORS OF TERRORISM FOR CLASHING WITH POLICE. This chair is the result of years of research and experimentation; it intersects between art and science. After dressing I walk around leisurely, deciding on shoes and earrings – there are so many nice things glittering in my jewellery box. POPE FRANCIS HEADS TO CUBA. It's difficult to choose between a light raincoat and a heavy scarf; I decide on a merino cardigan: the best of both worlds. You can motivate millennial employees by putting pictures of cute cats around the office. There is a full day of meetings ahead; I reply to five emails while eating half a cup of muesli with a cut-up pear. SEE KATE MIDDLETON'S EXCITING NEW LOOK.

Arranged marriages don't always work for animals in captivity. We're going to have lunch at the fish markets near my work. Why do women love to read about love? I put my dishes into the kitchen sink and fill up my thermos with fresh ginger tea. TIPS ON HOW TO PARENT WHEN YOU'RE BROKEN-HEARTED. Watch this spider turn wasps into mummified cowboys. I walk out of the stained-glass front door, headed for the bus stop. DEBRIS FOUND AT THE BOTTOM OF THE SEABED IS BELIEVED TO BE ATLANTIS. The bus going into town flashes past me at the lights and I cuss into the wind. This sticky lemon chicken is the perfect dinner party dish. I don't want to wait for another bus. HENRI MATISSE WAS BORN ON THIS DAY IN 1869. In a dream last night, two lions slept on either side of me while I sunbathed in the middle of the road. NIGERIAN PRESIDENT GATHERS SOLID EVIDENCE OF OIL CORRUPTION. It was the main road, this one right outside my house, lined with leaning trees.

WHISTLEBLOWER EDWARD SNOWDEN TALKS ALIEN ENCRYPTION. What is cry editing in music videos? I have an Oral-B electric toothbrush; I'm convinced it gives my teeth a superior clean. Does Xi Jinping care what America thinks of China? After brushing my teeth, I wash my face with Clean & Clear Morning Burst. A NEW GEOLOGICAL STUDY MAY EXPLAIN HOW HAWAI'I WAS FORMED. I like the tiny orange beads and how the face-wash builds into a gentle foam. ISRAELI AIRCRAFT HIT TARGETS IN GAZA AFTER ROCKETS ARE FIRED ON A TOWN. In an unfair world, only the young and rich can thrive. I pull out the top drawer and try to find my favourite aqua bra, a gift to myself last Christmas. HUNGARY ACCUSES MIGRANT PROTESTORS OF TERRORISM FOR CLASHING WITH POLICE. This chair is the result of years of research and experimentation; it intersects between art and science. After dressing I walk around leisurely, deciding on shoes and earrings – there are so many nice things glittering in my jewellery box. POPE FRANCIS HEADS TO CUBA. It's difficult to choose between a light raincoat and a heavy scarf; I decide on a merino cardigan: the best of both worlds. You can motivate millennial employees by putting pictures of cute cats around the office. There is a full day of meetings ahead; I reply to five emails while eating half a cup of muesli with a cut-up pear. SEE KATE MIDDLETON'S EXCITING NEW LOOK. This afternoon I'm meeting with the family who adopted my child. Arranged marriages don't always work for animals in captivity. We're going to have lunch at the fish markets near my work. Why do women love to read about love? I put my dishes into the kitchen sink and fill up my thermos with fresh ginger tea. TIPS ON HOW TO PARENT WHEN YOU'RE BROKEN-HEARTED. Watch this spider turn wasps into mummified cowboys. I walk out of the stained-glass front door, headed for the bus stop. DEBRIS FOUND AT THE BOTTOM OF THE SEABED IS BELIEVED TO BE ATLANTIS. The bus going into town flashes past me at the lights and I cuss into the wind. This sticky lemon chicken is the perfect dinner party dish. I don't want to wait for another bus. HENRI MATISSE WAS BORN ON THIS DAY IN 1869. In a dream last night, two lions slept on either side of me while I sunbathed in the middle of the road. NIGERIAN PRESIDENT GATHERS SOLID EVIDENCE OF OIL CORRUPTION. It was the main road, this one right outside my house, lined with leaning trees. I just lay there naked as cars moved around me.

X

O,

Just got to Sydney. Sorry about last night. Miss you all the time. The tears weren't planned. Thanks for the peppermint tea. When you opened the door it felt like coming home. Sorry to leave. Seems like I'm always leaving. To be fair, I leave everyone. Ask my mother. Or my brother. Ask the bank. I just take off.

X,

A broken heart doesn't go with any of my adventure clothes. I got some new Nikes for the gym and three Kathmandu jackets that I wear for walking and half a dozen pairs of gym tights that make my butt look pretty good. Basically, my life is one big adventure!

I went to Athlete's Shoes because they had a sale and the woman almost convinced me to get these ugly sneakers that were actually quite practical and probably would've been better for my flat arches.

I walked up Mt Eden last week. There were lots of tourists at the top taking selfies. I thought about you a couple of times.

O,

Just landed in Kuala Lumpur. I sat next to an Asian gang on the plane. They were wearing knee-high platform boots with large metal spikes. I wonder how they got through customs and why my lip-gloss looked so much more menacing to the customs officers?

Being with you was a lot like stargazing. I was in awe but never really part of it.

X,

Stargazing isn't how I'd describe it – that's a bit filmic.

I'd say it was more like dating a psychopath. Jokes! Don't beat yourself up too much, plenty of fish in the sea and all that. Maybe you should come with a warning though – like how they have those sickly pictures on cigarette packets? "WARNING: Dating this woman may lead to insomnia, lack of appetite and reduced libido."

O,

Haha. Very funny. You might be onto something though... I think I did you a favour. Clearly I'm flammable.

X,

Take care. I'm going on a Tinder date tonight. She's a nurse like a kids' nurse?

I hope you're getting out there too. I don't know what dress to wear. Fuck it, I might just rock up in my gym clothes.

O,

I wanted to say Merry Christmas last month and then didn't and then regretted it and then wasn't sure if that was the right thing to do. I also wrote to you a fortnight ago, on the 12th of January to be precise, but went through a similar process. I wanted to let you know that Mere died. I didn't come home for the funeral.

The house is just how she left it, nobody else in the family wanted Tiger so they gave him to the SPCA. I left a box of our things in the wardrobe upstairs. Love letters, lube, bullets and the black dildo. The key is still in the gumboot near the back door, would you please go and retrieve them before my mum inevitably does a clean out?

London is cold and Brixton is freezing. The egg-white walls don't look as good in winter. My flatmates have all changed but my job is the same. I'm still in Clapham trying to sell snow to the Eskimos. Sometimes I think about you on my lunch break.

You never said how your date went? Did you hit it off with the nurse?

X,

We went to see a movie and it was just my luck that she has some kind of undiagnosed condition? She couldn't stop talking and humming during the film, it was fucked up. Why do I attract crazy women? Am I going around with a sign on the back of my head that says something like 'Are you severely unhinged? If so, get at me!' So no, still single and still on Tinder. I've been on a few dates but haven't met anyone special. How about you - are you seeing anyone? A therapist, at least? Lol.

I'm so sorry about Mere. She was a brilliant woman. If you need to talk we can skype? Did she leave you the house? I'll go and find the box (the *black box* lol!). That is if your mum hasn't already taken the dildo out to use on her boyfriend. God, he's a bore. Are they still seeing each other? I hope she's giving it to him up the ass right now, haha!

O,

Mum is marrying him! They seem to get on okay and he's nice enough but I don't like his children. One of his daughters - the obese one - she's on some kind of volunteering OE teaching at kindergartens across Africa. I saw a photo of her in Zanzibar surrounded by cute black kids. She looked like a swollen lobster. Is it bad that I hope she'll be torched and eaten by the locals? She could feed an entire village.

Don't joke about Mum using our sex toys. It's actually giving me nightmares just imagining her taking the lid off that box.

X,

What did you do with the harness?

O,

I gave it to my brother.

X,

Oh, he's a good sport.

Finally got around to Mere's last night. It was weird. The beds were made upstairs and the kids' toys were out – like she was expecting your dad and his sisters to come home from school? How was she towards the end?

She left cake tins on the bench next to a packet of dried dates and a jar filled with spare change. I thought the hint was something like 'Make a sticky date cake!' I baked a huge one last night and took it to work this morning. Most of my colleagues have stopped eating sugar so it was a hard sell.

I'm getting pretty sick of tutoring and starting to think about moving to Melbourne. A friend of mine just opened a café in Brunswick. I could work there until I find something better. I don't know what 'better' would be at this point.

I threw out the dildo on my way home from Mere's, just chucked it into a random bin at Mission Bay. Stopped for a bit to put my feet in the water and have a smoke.

O,

The last time I saw Mere we had ravioli for dinner and she was perfectly herself, just a bit wheezy and tired. I think she had two glasses of red wine? I'm glad you followed her orders and made cake.

I'm staying at Dad's estate on the weekends an hour outside of London. He's got tenants in the main house but they don't mind having me here. I told him I wanted to start my own digital agency so he thinks I'm coming up with a business plan and trying to design a website. Actually it's just nice to have space to paint – oh yeah, I've started doing my art again. I haven't seen any of my old friends from boarding school, thank God.

Should you ever come and see me: (obviously fly to Heathrow first, yada yada) catch a train from Waterloo to Woking. Make sure you get a fast train where Woking is the first or second stop. (Woking is usually the first stop for trains going to Portsmouth.)

Get bus 462 or 423 leaving from outside the train station and going towards Guilford (numbers alternate so it will be one or the other). Try and plan the train around the bus times as I find Woking to be one of the lower points of civilisation.

Bus times are:
1550
1620
1730
1825
1925 (last one)

It's important to leave the train station from the right side otherwise it will be much more difficult to find the bus. I think you should arrive at platform 2, in which case you will need to take the stairs and cross over to other side of track, but if in doubt ask someone. All the busses leave from a road the runs beside the train station, under a large canopy. When you come out of the station look to the right and you can't miss them.

Get off the bus at Burntcommon roundabout. It will take

about 30-40 mins depending on traffic but ask the driver to be sure, they are usually lovely. The stop is just after the petrol station.

It's unlikely, but you never know.

X,

It's *highly* unlikely, but just for shits and giggles what's the petrol station I should look out for?

O,

Shell, of course.

X,

Do you need anything from the shop there, milk or bread?

O,

Yes, please. It's a limited selection but if you can – I like the decent orange juice with pulp, in the fridge beside the milk and cheese. If they've run out of that just bring sparkling water – oh, and they have wine too! There's a fluorescent pink rosé that you should avoid at all costs.

X,

So a bottle of neon rosé then? Check.

Patriarch, Eldest Son, *Ghost Son, Daughter*

She was 14.

And you were what, 15?

Hold on, she was 13.

Was she beautiful?

I was 16.

16! You know what they'd call you these days?

A ladies' man?

A sex offender.

I was the same age as her in my head.

Did Mum know about this?

I doubt it.

What would I tell her for?

You always told us kids that she was your first love.

Yeah, first love don't mean first girlfriend.

I'm just shocked.

You're a good boy, son.

He's a cold-blooded lawyer...

Why are you telling us this?

Because he's dying, stupid.

Because of memories.

Remembering your sins?

Remembering my life.

Rebecca, hello – anyone home?

I'm just processing things.

Don't you think it's a bit gross?

Yeah, I guess so. It's a bit of a surprise, Dad.

When I first came from Samoa, I got a job up north working on a farm. They had different ways up there.

So it was normal to carry on like that?

Give him a break.

It was a different time.

Can I give these crackers to the kids?

Help yourself, love. Where are they?

Watching TV in the whanau room, I'll be back in a minute.

Just stay, dear, hold on. We had a baby... but it was dead.

A stillborn?

A blue boy.

Yes.

With the girl, the 13-year-old?

She was a woman in my eyes.

Where did you bury the baby?

I don't know.

You don't know?

Son, pass me another pillow?

Is it your neck, Dad? I can get a nurse...?

You want us to look for the girl or something? Would she still be alive?

It's just... I'm dying, and I'm scared because that baby will be waiting for me on the other side. Maybe it hates me.

You're talking nonsense. That baby would've gone to heaven a long time ago.

You would've thought so, eh sis?

How did you meet her?

I asked her to come with me to a dance and she said yes.

You were allowed out dancing at 13 and 16?

No, I wasn't 16, I was about 16, 17... 18. She got in easy because she looked a lot older.

18? Bloody hell, Dad.

The twins are asking for something sweet – are you going to eat these bananas?

Here take them, sis.

Take the whole bag, dear, and the lemonade too.

They're fine with water but I'll take the grapes.

Bring them in if you want. There're plenty of chairs.

Let them play, Dad.

It's all right; they're watching cartoons and drawing. They're fine.

Okay, dear.

Did she work on the same farm as you?

Who?

The girl!

He's not thick. You don't have to yell!

I can hear you – my ears work. Yes, the girl worked on the farm. Stop pacing, come and sit down, son.

Let him pace – lawyers always pace. You've seen the TV shows, Dad.

It's just a lot to take in. I thought you and Mum... I don't know what I thought.

I loved your mother. The one up north was different.

She was 'different' how?

She was up in the hills taking care of her dad. He'd gone a bit funny in the head after the wife passed.

Do you know where they are now?

The dad would've died a long time ago.

I meant the girl... well – the woman, and the boy.

I never said anything about a boy.

Yes, you did, heaps of times after you'd been drinking.

It was before you met mum, there's nothing to be ashamed of Dad.

I'm not ashamed. It's just a long time since I thought about these things.

Great. I just caught the twins at the vending machine. Did you give them money, Dad?

No, sweetheart.

I gave them a few dollars when I got here. What – your boys allergic to sugar or something?

You know I don't like them eating crap.

He didn't mean any harm, love.

Sorry for spoiling my nephews. Won't happen again. I'll wrap them coal at Christmas, shall I?

Typical. See you soon, Dad – I'm taking the kids across the road for dinner.

You should go home and get some rest.

There's an Italian place, they'll have pizza or something.

Okay, love. You coming back after?

Just for a quick kiss goodnight. Do you want anything, Dad?

Honestly, he's fine. Don't come back – you're exhausted. Go home and sleep.

My dinner's coming soon. I'm fine, love. See you soon.

Sorry about the sweets, sis. Next time I'll bring them celery sticks and carrots.

Ha, very funny! Don't let Dad wander off – they'll be around soon to take his blood pressure.

Yes, boss!

Be nice – she's the one who's been looking after me.

We can't all be saints.

Am I going to see my eldest grandson before I die?

He'll drop in after school tomorrow. Polyfest is next month – they've got live-ins every weekend. He's just busy. It's a full schedule for the boy.

Too busy to call?

I'll make sure he visits tomorrow, Dad.

Waste of space.

Oh, good. I'm looking forward to seeing him.

Are you really dying, Dad? The doctors don't know everything. We should get a second opinion. Better yet, let's go private – I'm happy to foot the bill.

Money can't buy everything, son. All I want is time with you kids.

Luckily I've got heaps of leave owing.

I had a dream last night. Your mother was in a boat – right here in this room above my head. It was floating!

I dream about her too sometimes. It doesn't mean you're done for.

She was calling my name but it sounded far away – like she was calling from outside in the car park.

Did she reach her hand down over the edge of the boat for you? Was it even her, or was it someone else in the boat and Mum was actually in the car park? Sounds confusing.

I saw her whole arm come down towards me and I was getting ready to climb into the boat, taking the plugs out of my chest.

You woke up, didn't you?

The doctors woke me up on morning rounds. My arms were up in the air!

Bet you looked crazy, Dad.

I can feel her close by.

And the boy you had up in the hills?

I can feel him, too.

Look, I'm happy to make some calls, try to track the family down. Some of her relatives will still be up there, I'd bet good money on it.

When you take my body home, son, it's going to be hard for you kids to understand the old ways.

You are home, and we're going to bury you in Mangere at the family plot next to Mum – but look, I really don't think it's your time. Hospitals make you feel sick because there's more germs here than sticking your head down a public toilet.

Men from the village, they'll be waiting there outside the house.

I think you're tired, Dad, and sick of eating hospital mush. It's making your brain soft.

You do look pretty tired, Dad.

They were waiting outside her house after he was born – my dad's brothers. They took him away.

Really? They drove all the way up north?

I'd moved into her house in the hills. The father was going mad so I helped the girl take care of him.

Papa appreciated you, even though he was mean-spirited.

But they found you miraculously? Sounds far-fetched.

My cousins were forced to tell them where I was.

So your uncles just turned up in the hills and drove off with your baby?

They came to the house thinking he was alive.

So they were always going to take him, no matter what?

I heard them shouting my name outside.

Were you scared?

I'd grown up around them so I wasn't scared, but she was.

Did her dad try and do anything?

He just sat in his room rocking back and forth.

So they came into the house and then what?

I gave the boy to them.

It was a rainy day. Muddy as hell.

What about the girl? She just handed him over?

She didn't have a say.

Why did they want him so badly?

We were kids ourselves, you know. I've had a lot of time to think about this, son, and they were just doing what they thought was best. Protecting the family.

Maybe they buried him in the family plot? Or he could have been cremated? Sent back to Samoa with an aunty? They sound pretty serious but I don't think they would've just dumped him.

See, that's the thing I didn't understand until you lot came along. Just... wondering, eh, where he was resting. In my heart there's sadness when I think of him alone in the ground.

If you knew what happened to him, do you think you'd be at peace?

Yes, then you kids could go and mark him - give him his name.

His name?

Tausani.

What does that mean?

The dawn chorus.

I was driven to the farm where you met my mother.

After they left, I walked to the farm.

They stopped the car and carried me to the end of the property, through a fence and down to the foot of a great kauri.

I went to the end of the property. It was raining and I felt sick. I leaned against the fence and looked at all the trees. There was a huge kauri.

They dug through the forest floor and into the soil. The last thing I felt was rain – great big droplets of rain landing on my eyelids.

I hung around there like a bad smell, feeling confused. It got darker and darker.

It got darker and darker.

CORNER OF BLEIBTREU

1

Corner of Bleibtreu appeared her. Glinted shop
window apostle. Die mauer message nexus. West bird
east kiss cascading *always*. Autumn transmutation.
Beat, iambic beats undress her.

2

Alligator child your mother is a crocodile. She lives
in the canal out every peach lit morning her gold teeth
flecking *please please help me!*

Heimat is a feeling. The word to pre-exist
commentary at university (Lockean proviso) native
Berlin cites land as instinct. Like most channels of the
mind, followed long enough all thoughts will meet.

3

Wild boar blue bird, dinosaur wall (brick) behold
wordless acorn drip.

I have stopped thinking I live inside my time.
Ferrying animated men and their lies and their charms
until the fore tide swoons. I have stopped time I live
inside my thinking.

4

The fog spends morning baptising new roads.
Granular transport system. Long division by pen
alludes to young women as only sea or field. Watery
bone.

There are no shortcuts. The line of the grid is
uncompromising. Little dreams little birds grown old. I
wrap my arms around shadows. Visiting saint in parole
orange stops for a smoke. I release the shadows.

There are no sob stories. The line of the grid will complete a circuit in usual time.

5

Words fall *fall* glossy hybrid moments.

We must return ourselves back inside colourless prisms, back inside lonely skin. Trying to stay friends with names. Trying to fall for thoughts.

The city is a forest wound about the brain plug, another site to forage long into the night, into the conscious river.

6

Loose footpath inspection by crumbling light. Appears, overcast brow march as though no horror organised itself. Seek sheepish elixir – find the mortar young.

I draw fresh blood into my palm, wade festive soil. Call the priestess to my room.

7

Conversation at Hauptbahnhof with my chosen father about girls who get their tits out for art, the pussy magnet. I want to know the other hand of time, where meanings can be measured.

Two trains to see James in Neukollner, I fritter endless entry points *a thesis?* God takes my hands in the garden; he says there is nothing left to sell.

8

Some nights I woke inside the wrong woman. She
wrote of drowning in measured loops. I have no real
sadness. You have pinned me to my shadow.

Some days I could not bear the shedding leaves. The
wrong woman put herself into my dress. I have no real
shadow. You have pinned me to my sadness.

9

Fruit flies stream. Landing southern currents. John's
emerald pe'a thrashes at the Turkish corner bar white
wine white cigarette ash. The boys won't tell me how to
walk home how to dip my voice into the blue night.

Every corpse comes with us. Blood swum
contemporary hostage I am no better than TV terror.
Ready, when my people throw their heads back. Howl.

10

I sit cushioned near the kitchen watching staff smile.
They wave to me cooking and cleaning.

The tables are covered in mandarin roses: Vincent
Gallo artist actor filmmaker! Axis of sex Axis of
presence. Deciding that was *all* she was. Momentary
lapse, open magazine across my lap. Neurological map
back into cerebral dowry.

11

We stroll to Manzini for bread and cheese, arm in
arm across metallic leaves.

Tiui knows the monsters I harbour. Home has
become an emotional membrane something that is not
desert. Inhale all the land has been. Think of how to go.

The field is a structure I hold in my mind.

A pair of famous German terrorists had a baby, on this street. The story goes. Tiui knows the monsters I harbour. Delicia, her parents remember that child.

12

The one punk of Charlottenburg sits on the same station handrail; he is clean, he is sentimental. He bows into his shadow when he begs.

13

Considering Europe's financial crisis, it was somewhere out in nowhere. I missed city lights and women plotting months with no sun. Remaining earth is country if you were born in the city.

She was gentle and drove all the way back to her nest. Past the new takeaway chain with burgers bigger than your head. Past the heart of Prenzlauer Berg with real drugs swimming around in her blood.

14

Preferring honesty to beauty has turned you into something unintended. I am infatuated with the promise of an ending. Negotiations of movement, both imaginary and ground ready, swoon under microscopes.

My hands hold a net of lemons; I go to Goltzstrasse for a synthetic feather. Lost, staring into bloody cirrus. Where is Mitte?

Where is the red-winged blackbird?

15

I saw a short dark man stuff his ribs into a bag, the bones shone scarlet for an instant.

Why are you suffering in the open? Asked another man, two of them in cream tracksuits on the way to a dentistry conference.

The short dark man just bled and bled, when he opened his mouth more blood came. He walked into a lake of leaves, covering himself in gold. He stood without a chamber for his heart.

16

The boys dry chocolate in the sun. I am no good with pigeons. The boys sleep in the Tiergarten guarded by the buffalo. I am no good with pigeons. The boys ascend the angel gate and light and smoke a field of sage. I am no good with pigeons.

The boys decide the city silently. The boys confuse my bed with rhetoric. The boys conjoin are kind awake, my flaws migrate. The boys gather my words between their beating wings.

17

In every painting there are mountains. In every building there are paintings. Spires of cream and the urgent pacific philosophising Saint Catherine, she was borne to heaven by angels afloat above the current, reminiscent of Andromeda in circular marble.

My people wrap cold elders in siapo; the cloth becomes the earthen wail *la teu le va sea nectar!*

18

Embossed indigenous coordinates, reef of cloud appropriated rhetoric. Why skylight A. exists, having filleted the ceiling. Corner of Ku'damm appeared her. Glinted shop window apostle.

She cries on the stage she cries on the train, when he looks down from heaven she tries to smile. I'm not concerned with in reality like-featured maidens water paddling lush distant as-where myths belong.

19

You dress as yourself before familiar forms, the warm machines battle your doubt, some use their cells to sing alone and will the air to rush. The forms give you life, about them you are yourself, you are leaning always into the air into a lover you are dressing always staying as yourself.

20

My naked reflection had become a bouquet in the night. Like lines ascending light her bare crevice under thinking palms. It was my naked mouth on earth. Her body had become me you, the convinced peering circle. No one great reflection.

Aunty Lupe tells me to keep a dream journal: 'Because it's going to unlock your unconscious, and help with everything sitting there at the back of your chest just waiting to pour out.'

I nod and take a long sip of my coffee, sweetened with organic sugar. All around her room I see different dreams that have run their course, plus a few still in bloom. Her latest collection of essays is stacked on a bookshelf beside an old photo of her parents that I've never seen. They look young, and convinced that they have a happy life ahead of them.

'Imagine a house,' she says. 'Say it's this place – where we're sitting right now. You're like this room, these yellow walls holding up the ceiling and giving something for the paintings to hang against and for the dog to bark at in the daytime while I write. But underneath the house there is a maze of concrete and earth, foundations covered in a million handprints. Do you kind of get what I'm trying to say, dear?'

I give her a smile and shake my head, admiring her halo – how does she get her frizzy hair to stay in place like that? When she smiles her eyes disappear and tiny piercing diamonds stare out. 'I don't know. I sort of understand.'

Aunty Lupe smiles back at me. 'That's the beauty of it. There are lots of things we don't know, and we don't have to – that's partly why we dream: to explore.' She leans back and gives herself an inward grin, claps her hands together and looks down at the morning tea between us. 'You don't like cheesecake?'

I take a slice and dig my fork into the wobbly centre of berry and biscuit, before bringing the cake to my lips and biting into it. She's pleased to see me eating something she chose all by herself; I have to finish the entire slice before we can resume our conversation. During my last mouthful she comes out of her trance.

'You've got to bargain with yourself,' Aunty Lupe says, 'like you do at work when you're talking to important people – I guess you do things like that sometimes, don't you? Tell yourself that after your meeting you can go to the staff kitchen and have a cup of tea and a break, even though you know deep down that you can't take a break until later in the day. It's the same thing with your dreams – if you make a commitment to write them down you'll find it easier over time to access your raw power. You won't just be the rooms and the roof. You'll know your foundations and what you're really made of.'

She runs both hands through her thick hair; a sweet and smoky smell uncoils from the roots – Port Royal and Red Door, cinnamon and black pepper, maybe loneliness and a tinge of mould creeping down from the ceiling.

'God, it makes your head swim when you draw a line in the sand between here and North America or here and Europe – truly the distance is astounding – but wherever *here* is, really think about it and make a deal with yourself to get beyond what exists, dear.'

Her golden retriever, Lucy, comes over and licks my foot; the silence between us grows and grows.

'I had this really weird dream last night,' I say. 'Actually, it was a sequence of dreams.'

'What happened?'

I collect my thoughts for a moment, remembering how sick I felt when I woke up in the middle of the night. 'Well,' I begin, shifting around in my seat, taking a long sip of the cold coffee beside me. 'I was in a glass apartment looking out from the living room right into another apartment building that was also made of glass, and it was only, say, five metres away from me. The other apartment was identical to the one I was in, except that it was full of people, some standing and some sitting. I recognised a few people and others were strangers. It was so close that I could see the freckles on their faces and the buttons they hadn't done up on their shirts. Some of them were holding babies in their arms and pointing at me as though I were a train or a fire truck. When I looked down at myself I realised I had no clothes on and I was crouched behind a coffee table.'

'Did you try to run? Did you scream out?' Aunty Lupe squeezes my hand.

'I screamed but they couldn't hear me because of the glass. I wanted to run but when I looked around I saw that the apartment was sealed off and there were no doors. It was weird, I felt trapped. I *was* totally trapped.'

'Did you wake up then?'

'Sort of – I woke up in another dream, I had a mouth full of blood and my back teeth were crushed to bits. I was worried about the cost of having them repaired but I couldn't stop playing with the exposed gum – no, playing is the wrong word. Exploring, I guess. It felt soft where the teeth had been, a bit like the cheescake.'

Aunty Lupe nods slowly, mumbling to herself as though consulting with an angel. 'Being naked in a dream, especially in front of a huge group of strangers, speaks to feelings of vulnerability in your physical life – is there anything going on at the moment that makes you feel a bit exposed?'

I spy a few romance novels on her bookshelf; the titles read like soft porn.

She catches my gaze and chuckles. 'It's research for a paper I'm writing on Pasifika sexuality. Books like that engage a lot of our people, old and young alike, they just won't admit it.'

The words 'our people' swirl around in my head. For a long time I knew exactly what that meant – it stood for everybody in the living room and the extra bodies lining the hallway. My mother always said that we moved as one great mass and that it didn't matter who got hurt or lost on the way as long as the group survived.

Aunty Lupe finishes the last of her coffee and reaches for my hand again. 'Are you okay, dear?'

'I woke up in a third dream, after I lost my teeth, only it wasn't a dream – it was a memory from when I was a girl. There were men taking my pyjamas off in the backyard and I could feel rain on my face and shoulders. It was night time, incredibly dark.'

Aunty Lupe looks to be in genuine pain. She chews on something imagined in her mouth. 'Who did that to you, sweetheart? I'm sorry, I would've done something if I'd been there...' Her eyes well up with tears, and her retriever whines in the corner. Aunty Lupe reaches into a packet of dog treats on the window – throwing a handful over her shoulder like confetti. Lucy runs over with her tail wagging.

'I didn't mean to upset you, Aunty Lupe,' I say, feeling bad that I've brought the cruel world with me into her villa. She loves being part of the retirement village; as well as the gardens and friendly neighbours there's a registered nurse on site seven days a week. While she drifts in and out of knowing who she is, the staff and other residents keep a close eye on her.

'You haven't upset me, petal, I just feel badly for you.'

'I couldn't see their faces because it was night time, but I remember them talking across me. There were a few different voices.' I look down at my hands and start pushing back my cuticles, then buffing my nails with the bottom of my shirt. 'They were over-stayers Mum had taken in. She probably thought she was doing the right thing. She *was* doing the right thing...'

'And that's how they repaid her kindness? Wherever those men are now, I can promise you they have terrible dreams – far worse than what you experienced last night. When you commit evil acts, that energy stays with you and it never lets go.'

'Honestly, I don't think about it very much, Aunty Lupe, and when I do it's all blurred, there's no pain.' I watch her soft hands fumble for a tissue from her pocket.

'You've blocked out the pain, sweetheart. There might be much more that you've chosen to leave in the past. You've done what you had to do to survive.' Aunty Lupe begins to cry, tears flowing down her face without a sound. 'Your mum never knew?'

She drifts off into a different moment; her face becomes very neutral and tired, the way my mother used to look when I was a girl coming home from school. She'd be in the kitchen with an apron around her waist covered in flour, banging drawers open and shut, looking for baking soda, cracking eggs open, flicking through the pages of a recipe book and running to the wash-house for cans of fruit that she stored in a cupboard above the sink. The house was full of hungry mouths and she took their hunger personally – it was an affront to the dream she had of living in the land of milk and honey. Her doors were open day and night. While my father worked a factory job in the day and pulled night shifts as a truck driver, my mother helped family, distant relatives and strangers to find their feet. It didn't matter that they were in the country illegally – she wasn't scared of dawn raids. What scared her was the oppression she'd left behind in the islands.

I shake my head at Aunty Lupe, 'No, Mum didn't know. I could never get the words out.'

'Are you angry, dear?'

'I might be, deep down, past all of the love and good memories.'

I look across and see that Aunty Lupe's gone to sleep; she does this often in her old age. I steel myself to lean across and breathe her in. The lines around her eyes are deep; she had tight olive skin in her youth but now everything has come away from the bone, and under her chin whiskers shine. On her right shoulder where her neck and back meet I draw a love heart. She doesn't respond.

I surprise myself and get up for another slice of cheesecake. She's put it away in the fridge beside a tiny jug of gin. It feels comforting to see that I still know all her tricks. I pour it down the drain, wondering where she gets it from, and artfully replace it with cold water. She won't know who did that when she wakes up, probably in a panic about another essay she's writing or the need to wipe down the walls and sweep her kitchen. I take a good look around her little home and feel good about all the money I've sunk into the place – she deserves some peace and fantasy in her old age. Lucy is curled up fast asleep next to the bookshelf.

Sunlight streams in through the bay window. All of the crooked paintings make me smile. Her dream journal is open on the coffee table; she's written my name at the top of a list entitled *Favourite People.*

A sliver of drool curls its way down her lip. She startles herself with a cough and wakes up, quickly rubbing her mouth clean. 'Are you going, my dear? Did I nod off? Oh, I'm sorry, love.'

I bend down beside her and make a funny face. 'I ate more of the cheesecake while you were asleep and it was delicious. Thank you for a lovely afternoon.'

She puts her arms around my waist; I go weak at the knees.

'Don't you worry,' she coos. 'We move as one great mass; it doesn't matter who gets hurt or lost on the way as long as the group survives.'

You got married. He proposed on time. Followed the deadline mentioned politely: *I'm in my mid-twenties. Is this going anywhere?*

I kept pretending I hadn't seen you at cafés and festivals, looking like you'd lost weight. I stopped following you on Facebook. Decided our lives had grown apart.

We never spent time walking around, swinging our arms the way other girls did. We never hung out, in ourselves, the way other girls did.

I remember being in Herne Bay surrounded by the atua and they were discussing something right over my head. The words felt like baby flies landing on my arms and legs. I couldn't catch anything, I couldn't relate to the mumbling.

When I see you drinking mineral water on the corner of Ponsonby Road you are more beautiful than I remember, and I realise the corner was always coming. Can you believe that our parents and their parents survived wars and fell in love on time and didn't die, just so you and I could to run into each other on this corner?

Can I be the old friend who mentions how different you sound? I was absolutely wrong about the voice in my head, cackling and poking holes. It turns out you've suffered too and I've probably given the wrong impression about immortality as though the one elixir is the one we can't discuss.

A lot of people around us are making money from making solutions for the reporting problems of organisations that are fat and lazy. We have a good laugh about knowing where we fit into that truth, and then you remember that I was never your friend.

I was a baby fly.

You open the door. He's cradling a cheap bottle of red as though it's a newborn babe. 'Sorry, suga, rehearsal ran late.'

Of course you don't believe him. Anyway you're more concerned with why his head is so pointy, the age gap, and the fact that he smokes like a chimney and smells like an ashtray. He beams when you move aside and let him in. You watch his taut dancer's body float towards the kitchen where you've prepared a light supper.

His voice booms, 'Wow, what a view. Shit, Maungawhau's right there – very nice, miss!'

He puts the wine down on the island bench and takes off his jacket. Something about the shape of his arms makes up for the vacancy behind his eyes. He smells like Dunhill Reds but there's another scent forcing its way through. 'Are you wearing cologne?' you ask. He nods, showing all his teeth, accepting the flute of bubbles you hand him effortlessly. Like clockwork, your bodies arrange themselves at the dining table across from each other. You pour the wine as he runs his hands over the varnished wood.

'Pretty mint table. Where'd you get it from?'

'Trade Me,' you chirp. 'Cheap as chips and free delivery too.'

He leans back and nods, letting out a sigh. 'It's Calvin Klein, the cologne. You like it? Thought I'd make an effort. To be honest I couldn't believe it when you answered my call.' Again the shark grin flashes.

You smile and reach for the prawns, chilli-specked on a bed of rocket; he's not the only one who's surprised. According to your New Year's resolutions, 25 meant yoga and career development, you declared that you'd had enough sorbet – your palate was officially refreshed and you were ready for a relationship.

'Far out, these prawns are yum. Who taught you how to cook?'

You watch him push the rocket leaves to the side of his plate as though he's allergic to salad. The prosecco takes hold and you pour another glass almost to the brim.

'I did something on my last trip to Samoa. Is it cool to show you?' he asks.

Maybe, you think to yourself, maybe his thoughts are so big and bold that there isn't enough room to house them in the usual circular chamber that's fitted to mere mortals. Perhaps that explains his weird pointy skull. He's probably some kind of legend reincarnated, like a warrior in the city.

He walks over to the windows and begins to let down the blinds. The night sky disappears, Mt Eden and K Road fall from view. He starts to talk in a low register. 'I know I was a boy the last time we hung out, but shit's changed. I'm a man now.'

If you're 25 and he's 38, that means he was a boy last year. So you were a child at 24, no less, an embryo. His shadow casts a huge figure against the red feature wall, and now that you know you're alone with no chance of anyone on the street looking up and seeing in, you begin to doubt yourself. Everything else in your life has just started to make sense – you joined the gym last week and you're on the blood type diet. It won't be long until all the puppy fat around your hips disappears.

'Okay, so close your eyes,' he says grinning.

The last time you closed your eyes on him, opening them again was like waking up in a sea of ash. White flecks everywhere, your neck resting on his chest. Head rising and falling with each of his breaths, wondering if you really were more powerful than him, something he repeated over and over again while he was inside you.

'All right, open them.'

He has his back to you, his pants are off, and his hands are up behind his head.

'Well?' he says. 'What do you think?'

He's been given a traditional pe'a, the ink transforming the loose canvas of his body into a force of nature. He turns to face you, gesturing to the front of his thighs: rows of intricate lines, shark teeth, slanted diamonds, blocks of shimmering night, emerald-tinged.

'It took twelve days. I was in the worst pain. Actually I thought about you a bit. I started to hallucinate and then I sort of heard your voice. That's why I called a bunch of times when I got back last month. Thinking about you made the pain go away.'

You cross your arms and concede, 'It's beautiful, really. I'm glad you got it done.'

'I wanted you to see for yourself that I've changed – like, literally.'

He walks towards you and takes off his shirt, dropping it on your new couch, another Trade Me score. 'I think stuff got a bit confused the last time we hooked up. I was drunk and a bit of a dick? But everything's different now – I'm not just dancing, I'm doing all this youth work too and looking after my nephews so my sister can go to night classes and get her degree. I want to get ahead like you.' He reaches out and touches your face with his huge hands. His mouth is cold and wet, opening and closing on your collarbone, with his fish tongue flicking aimlessly. You begin to remember his obsession with necks, how it felt as though he was trying to paint you with his saliva last time. He brushes your fringe from your face exactly like the rocket salad on his plate. His fingers force their way across your lips. You want to bite them, you want to taste them, but none of it's the way you imagined at the supermarket: getting the frozen prawns, putting them back, throwing sirloin into the trolley, changing your mind and putting it back. You're happy you didn't cook him steak – he was so late it would've been cold anyway, and part of you wants to treat him badly simply because you can. That's why you didn't buy fresh prawns. Maybe it doesn't matter if he's helping his sister.

Your stomach turns for a second and the apartment seems to spin. 'Hold on,' you say, moving out from his grip and walking across to the couch, sitting down and collecting yourself. 'I just need a minute.'

He doesn't seem annoyed. His muscular shadow sits down naked on the Barcelona chair by the window, and then there's the glow of his phone as he checks his emails and starts to whistle. 'I'm all good here. You just have your moment, babe.' He flops back and brings the phone right up to his face; you can see his muscles rippling while he opens up Candy Crush.

Who cares if you have a real connection, right? Aren't all couples different? Isn't it true that opposites attract? Anyway you're not a couple and that's the point of a booty call, casual sex, friends with benefits – that's what modern women are doing all over the world. Screwing beautiful men who are clearly just for looking at – not for debating politics with or discussing the meaning of life. He's kindle to keep the fire burning until you meet your *soul mate*. Perhaps it will be refreshing to be with someone who lives inside his body and not up in his head like you. Complicated you, with a brand-new, gold-framed mirror from Trade Me (another bargain) that you just can't bring yourself to hang anywhere in the apartment because nowhere feels quite right. The poor thing sits slanted at the end of the couch; it's only useful for looking at your shoes in the morning before you go to work. You're starting to dislike yourself for having a treasure that you keep buried for fear of bad feng shui.

You turn towards the island with a plan to scrub the stove top and benches for the third time this evening, only to feel his hands suddenly around your waist and his hot breath blasting the back of your neck. This is something else you thought of at the supermarket while going through the self-service checkout. You imagined his strong hands digging into your sides, bending you over the dining table and fucking you from behind. As you scanned hummus and apple juice, turning the items slowly and waiting for the machine to beep, you saw yourself splayed open, maybe in ecstasy, maybe clouded by a certain shame.

He leans into you, pressing softly at first in time with his kisses, until his hands are pulling down your tights and the ugly granny panties you chose to keep yourself from taking them off. 'I just want to say...' you start.

He mutters nonsense, turning you around and drowning his face in your breasts, pinning you to the closest wall.

'So we're, like, obviously attracted to each other but I don't know if there's an intellectual connection?'

He lifts your linen dress up over your head; you raise your arms and feel relieved when he undoes your bra and pulls down your knickers. Everything lightens. It isn't an exam or an essay that needs footnotes with masses of academic citations, you aren't *lesser than* for wanting something that makes no sense.

And then he's whispering like a man possessed, 'Have my son, let's make our son. He'll be strong like me and smart like you.' His pointy head gently makes its way down between your thighs. You try to smooth the edges of his temples, convincing yourself that he'd look perfectly normal with a hat. His fish tongue is lost in the bridge of flesh between your vagina and your buttocks. He swears into your pubic hair, *Oh, fuck... such a nice pussy... oh, fuck...*

You open your eyes and look around at all your beautiful things. The second-hand dining table with a beaded Indian runner, the marble island with a sophisticated stack of cookbooks including gluten-free and vegan options, the Taylor guitar in the corner of the room that you strum to yourself some nights. His tongue finds its way inside you, thrashing deeper and deeper.

And that's when you decide on the perfect place to hang the gold mirror.

CHARACTERS

April
Grandpa
Ios
Petrol station guy

LOCATIONS

Auckland airport
Grandpa's car
Petrol station
Family home

TIME PERIOD

Not so long ago

TEMPO

Allegro, to be played with feeling

COMMENTS

They really *do* reunite by the downstairs McDonald's at Auckland Airport. April is quite self-absorbed so don't believe her when she says she's overcome.

April should be played by a male in his twenties and Grandpa should be a petite Tahitian woman wearing pearls. Ios should bark because he's a glorious bullmastiff.

NB: Grandpa is always in a hurry because he has a weak bladder. Ios should be as close to tall dark and handsome as possible.

Act 1
April returns from Berlin

April is shitting herself, she spelt her name wrong on the 'nothing to declare' form. She feels stupid. Such an amateur mistake – what the hell is all that 'self-development' worth if you can't write your own fucking name? This is an issue. Walking through the arrivals gate, she starts to worry that she's picked up early onset dementia from over exposure to antique shops. Who are all the gloves for? Her love of vintage leather is the kiss of death; truly her bank account suffers for it. Her grandfather appears in a Lion Red vest and her cousin Ios walks past, looks right through her. Oh yes! The poverty diet worked! She is dusty and poor, but thin! Hurrah! They come together by the downstairs McDonald's, Grandpa has an air of impatience and Ios is wearing silver Dirty Dog sunglasses inside. It's almost midnight. Hurrah!

IOS: Say something?

APRIL: I'm April?

IOS: Fail. You still sound like a Kiwi.

GRANDPA: Good to see you, dear. Now you're safe, girl. There are too many terrorists nowadays.

APRIL: What about when I say *bitte shoen*? And, I love *currywurst*!

April glares at Ios.

I've missed you, Grandpa. Thank you for coming to get me.

IOS: Verse? Versed who?

GRANDPA: You want a coffee, dear?

APRIL: Don't worry, I'll make one at home, Grandpa. I'm just so overcome.

GRANDPA: Take those things off, son, it's midnight.

Ios removes his sunglasses and flexes his muscles.

APRIL: Currywurst is just curry powder on cut up sausages with a bit of bread. You'd like it, Ios.

GRANDPA: You ate a lot of German foods over there then, dear?

IOS: I wouldn't eat that crap.

GRANDPA: It's good to give new things a go. Like the Asians, son. They need to give Kiwi life a proper go.

APRIL: I've seen you eat brains, Ios. And Grandpa, about the racism – I thought you'd grown out of it?

Act 2
Grandpa complains

Grandpa is in the front seat of his car, shaking his head and panting. He feels hot and cold all at once, he wants to use the bathroom and he misses his wife (also all at once). April sits in the passenger seat with a blank stare. Ios has put his sunglasses back on. His long day at work has caught up with him and he's very irritable. They take a while to find the exit to the carpark; Grandpa complains the whole way into town.

GRANDPA: $12, those bloody bastards!

APRIL: Who?

IOS: The airport carpark.

GRANDPA: Costs the bloody earth to park here!

APRIL: It's cheaper than Heathrow.

IOS: Unhelpful, cuz.

APRIL: You'll find out one day, if you ever leave home...

GRANDPA: Could've bought a whole pig with that!

They turn out of the carpark onto the main road.

IOS: You get me anything from Duty Free?

APRIL: Some free cologne samples – they were giving them out.

GRANDPA: Next time, dear, you catch the bus.

APRIL: There won't be a next time. Well, not for a while.

IOS: Really? You said that last year. Heartbreaker.

APRIL: God, Ios, do you still think I killed Aunty Belle?

IOS: Just weird that you rang, said something, then *boom*!

GRANDPA: I'm putting a curse on that carpark: a plague of fleas on you arseholes!

APRIL: I told her I missed her, that's all! I was half-suffocated by sadness.

IOS: Yeah, see? Broke her old heart in two.

Act 3
April fills the tank

Ios waits in the car while April goes into the petrol station to pay for petrol and Grandpa goes in to use the bathroom. April has a cryptic encounter with the guy who works there. He likes her straight away but the feeling isn't mutual. The petrol station smells like fish. April has an 'aha' moment.

PETROL STATION GUY: You aren't a local. I'd remember your face.

APRIL: I've been overseas for a while.

PETROL STATION GUY: Yeah, you have a bit of an accent.

APRIL: Did you realise that it smells like fish in here?

PETROL STATION GUY: It doesn't smell like fish in here!

He flares his nostrils and breathes in deeply.

APRIL: You might just be used to it, the fish smell. The way my mum says people get used to the elephant house. At first it stinks but then your senses adjust and all you notice is the elephant.

PETROL STATION GUY: I'm not an animal person.

They're both silent for a moment.

If you can only notice the elephant, what does the elephant notice?

APRIL: Well, I guess the African bush elephant notices the African bush, and the African forest elephant notices the forest and the Asian elephant notices Asia.

PETROL STATION GUY: But an elephant in the elephant house is a house elephant, so it can only notice the elephant house?

APRIL: Aha!

Act 4
April chats with the kitchen sink

The kitchen window is slightly ajar; all of the dogs in the neighbourhood are asleep. April sits down at the kitchen table with a glass of milk and a pair of vintage gloves at her elbow. There are family photos on the closest wall and lots of mismatched patterns and fabric (the curtains and the wallpaper clash). You can hear a variety of snoring and the loud buzz of the fridge; she discusses a recent premonition with herself.

APRIL: So there you are, right where I left you.
'New Zealand *you*.' The same oily hair and the same dramatic
80s leather. It doesn't suit you it – doesn't suit anyone. The
eighties have been and gone. Sharks can't swim backwards;
it's time to embrace the new century. If you stay still, your
thoughts will marble all the way through like the spotless
white rock of the Taj Mahal.

I had a premonition, on the second flight home. I saw
myself ten years from now, 39 years old, surrounded by cats.
The ginger one wouldn't stop mewing so I kicked her away,
she left me with a mob of black cats and they swallowed
me up into their dark fur, a tornado of matted thorns. I was
everywhere in tiny droplets, a luscious, ruby plume. And you
were there 'New Zealand you' saying, 'I told you so, I warned
you, it's dangerous to follow your heart...'

April puts on the vintage gloves and drinks the glass of milk.

ACKNOWLEDGEMENTS

With special thanks to:

My manuscript advisor and dear friend, Lloyd Jones

My much-loved parents, Kim Meredith Melhuish and
Kingsley Spargo Melhuish

My publishers and aiga, Sally Greer, Kitki Tong and
Kyle Ranudo

Janet McAllister, Lesley Marshall, Jill Rawnsley,
Makerita Urale, Paula Morris, Robert Sullivan

Rosanna Raymond, John Daly-Peoples,
Layla Tweedie-Cullen

Nicola Shepheard, Tusiata Avia, Peter Bowden

My brothers, Cyrus Sebastian and Pelemoni Francis

And last, but not least, Miles